a MONTH WITH APRIL-MAY

When April-May February wins a bursary to the ultra-posh Trinity College she soon finds herself isolated as the scholarship kid and locked in a power struggle with the infuriating Mrs Ho. Will April-May get to keep her new and only best friend? Will her useless father Fluffy ever get round to washing her school uniform? And will Sebastian the hot boy-next-door ever notice her?

A Month with April-May, by bestselling South African author Edyth Bulbring, is the wonderfully funny tale of April-May's trials and tribulations as she navigates a new school, a new family, and a whole new way of life.

April-May! I'm super excited about your next book.'
Megan, The Book Addicted Girl

'The minute I began reading I did not want to stop, and finished the book in a few hours. Edyth Bulbring has taken a normal schoolgirl with everyday problems and turned her into an intriguing, quirky character that I needed to know more about. *A Month with April-May* is a quick read that I thoroughly enjoyed from the moment I began, but one that also ended far too soon, and I can't wait to see what happens next.'
Michelle, Much Loved Books

'April-May is a witty, funny character who is absolutely bursting with attitude . . . this was a speedy and amusing read which grabbed my attention from start to finish. I do look forward to seeing what April-May gets up to in her next instalments!'
Steph, Stepping Out of the Page

'April-May February has a special charm as does *A Month with April-May*. The novel made me smile and I loved April-May's "Cold Facts". I thought the last line of the novel was very meaningful.'
M & Little M, We Sat Down

Other praise for Edyth Bulbring

A Month with April-May

'I devoured the book in one sitting, but it passed the acid test when my teenage daughter was seduced by Bulbring's wit and humour, and was compelled by the sheer excellence of the writing to keep reading.'
The Times (South Africa)

100 Days of April-May

'Hilarious . . . Edyth Bulbring has proved wildy popular, so much so that her books are part of the syllabus for Grades 8 and 9 at a few schools [in South Africa].'
The Times (South Africa)

'Devoured in an evening and highly recommended.'
Media Update, South Africa

'One word: WOW! I absolutely loved this book! . . .The instant I read the very first word on the ivory page I was hooked . . .'
The Bookaholic Blog

The Summer of Toffie and Grummer

'If you love reading emotional and yet exciting stories, this book is for you. A true definition of a real emotional rollercoaster ride.'
Youth Village Online Magazine, South Africa

a Month With APRiL-MAY

EDyTH BuLBRiNG

HOT
KEY
BOOKS

First published in Great Britain in 2013 by Hot Key Books
Northburgh House, 10 Northburgh Street, London EC1V 0AT

First published by Penguin South Africa in 2010

A CIP catalogue record for this book is available from the British Library.

ISBN: 978-1-4714-0029-2

1

Typeset by Palimpsest Book Production Limited, Falkirk, Stirlingshire
This book is set in 11.25pt Fairfield LH Light

Printed and bound by Clays Ltd, St Ives Plc

Hot Key Books supports the Forest Stewardship Council (FSC), the leading
international forest certification organisation, and is committed to printing only
on Greenpeace-approved FSC-certified paper.

www.hotkeybooks.com

Hot Key Books is part of the Bonnier Publishing Group
www.bonnierpublishing.com

For Dr Ida Bell, and teachers like her

In my experience, there are two kinds of teachers in this world.

The first bunch barely make it out of bed to come to school. If they do pitch up for class, they can't teach for toffee, so they let you do exactly as you please. They don't know your name and they never show up for teacher–parent evenings. They're the best. I can deal with this lot.

The other crowd consists of people you just don't want hanging around your classroom. They give you assignments and expect you to do stuff like research. They want you to learn things. And they want you to enjoy it. They're always asking stupid questions and trying to interfere in your life. They are teachers like Mrs Ho. I should have known from the first moment I met her: it was either me or Mrs Ho. One of us was going to have to go.

One

I knew Mrs Ho was bad news on my first day at Trinity College. I don't know her name when I first meet her, but I've met the type before: uptight, pushy, at school before the first bell has stopped ringing.

I'm in the corridor between classrooms – ten minutes into my first day at my new school and I'm lost. She's yelling at me. Loudly. Like I'm deaf.

'What do you call this?' She shakes my school bag in the air. My lunch box falls out into the passage, followed by my polony rolls.

I want to tell her that it's my school bag, but I'm on my hands and knees, trying to get the stuff off the floor and away from the sniggers of three boys who are looking at my polony rolls like I'm trying to smuggle hand grenades into the school.

'Blue.' She shakes my bag. 'Not red and purple.' She points at my multicoloured satchel in disgust. 'Navy blue.

1

Those are the rules. Don't let me see this bag at school again.'

She tosses my bag down and is just about to stalk off when she sees my legs. From the expression on her face I think I've been amputated at the knees. Like paralympic runner Oscar Pistorius, except I don't have cool blades to help me bounce off to a gold medal and freedom.

'Stand up, girl.'

I stand up and her glare takes in my green-and-white striped socks.

'Do you think you're in the circus?'

I shake my head. Of course I don't think I'm in the circus. I'm at school.

'Take those off immediately.' She points at my socks.

She watches while I take off my shoes and socks and then put my shoes back on. I can walk around without socks all term until I get the regulation navy-blue ones. She says this and then leaves me sitting in the corridor, plotting how I can smother her to death with the polony that's fallen out of my rolls and on to the floor.

This teacher's trouble. I recognise the signs. I put her face at the top of my hit list.

I finally find my classroom and hobble inside, only to get allocated a desk at the back of the room with the class mouth-breather. Her name is Melanie and she goes out of her way to make me feel welcome. She breathes her boiled-egg breakfast all over me and whispers how pleased she is to have a desk-mate at last. She sat alone all last year. Why am I not surprised?

My seat with Melanie at the back of the class at Trinity College will be my home for my Grade Eight year. Home? This school's more like a prison. Blood-red walls tortured by ivy creep three floors up to a clock tower looming over a quad, its round face spying on the kids below, tick-tocking away the hours of our captivity.

Fluffy says if I mess up and don't perform to my potential he's giving me back to my mother.

Fluffy is my dad. It's just the two of us. There used to be three of us before Mom and Fluffy decided last year that they couldn't stand the sight of each other and split. They couldn't split me in half so Fluffy got to keep me. I'm not sure which of them thinks they got the better deal.

Melanie is the class monitor. She gives me some textbooks and stationery and says that all the books have to be covered in brown paper and plastic. These are the rules at Trinity College.

She also tells me that our classroom teacher is a man called Mr Goosen. But everyone calls him 'Finger'. I can see why when he comes into the room and takes roll-call for the day. As he calls out each name he looks up and then points, just to make sure that the voice and the face match the name on the clipboard. His index finger is missing in action so he points with his middle finger.

Finger comes to the end of the names and points his finger at Melanie. No, he's pulling the zap sign at me.

'April-May February.'

That's me.

My list of people who deserve to be poisoned with a side dish of salmonella is historically topped by Fluffy and Mom. Mr and Mrs February should have called it quits the day I was born, when they couldn't agree on what to call me. Fluffy thought April was the prettiest time of the year. Mom liked May. I got called a calendar.

Finger's middle finger wavers as he reads out my name for a second time. I stand up and stare that finger down. 'They call me Bella.' I nod encouragingly and hold nickies behind my back. I'm in the middle of reading *Twilight*, the first fang-bang novel by Stephenie Meyer, and I think Bella will do just fine. If I'd been a boy I would have gone for Edward.

Finger nods and lowers his finger. 'We have a new girl. Let's all clap hands and welcome April-May February to the school.'

He's obviously a slow learner.

After the class has given me a slow clap, Finger says he's got some urgent things to do and we must get on with whatever it is he's supposed to be teaching us. It's

4

History. We must read the first two chapters from the textbook and then discuss what we have read among ourselves. Quietly.

Melanie tells me that Finger doubles up as the History teacher. He's also the Deputy Principal and has been around since the ark was built. He's hanging in at Trinity College until he turns a century, then he'll get his pension and go and open a B & B in Clarens – a village near Bethlehem in the Free State (as opposed to Bethlehem in the Middle East).

I spend the next two hours reading *Twilight* while the rest of the class text each other. I don't have a cellphone. I think I'm the only teenager in Jozi who isn't connected. Oh, and Melanie, who says her phone fell into the swimming pool yesterday. I tell her cellphones are last month's monomania of the mediocre. I'm waiting for my new BlueBerry. Melanie sounds interested. Her father has a BlackBerry.

BlueBerry, BlackBerry, what's the diffs? Melanie says she can't see the diffs at all. Then she paints her finger-nails with Tipp-Ex and scratches it off with a safety pin. It's like dandruff all over my desk.

Finger comes back when the double lesson is almost over to check that no one's bunked off. He tells us to carry on reading from the textbook for homework and to think about History and things. I reckon he belongs to the first category of useless teachers. Finger can stay.

The next lesson is English. Call me a dork, or Boring Bella or whatever makes your cellphone whistle, but English is my favourite subject. The rest of the subjects can eat sand.

Melanie tells me that our English teacher is Miss Morape, who is sweet and loves Stephenie Meyer. Instantly I know Miss Morape is going to love me too. She is going to love me and leave me and *Twilight* in peace.

I begin rethinking our new best-friend status because the woman who walks into the classroom can't possibly be Miss Morape. She is not sweet. She can't love Stephenie. She's the one on top of my hit list. It is she who banned my multicoloured school satchel and has caused my feet to sweat blisters into my school shoes. 'Ho-ho-ho,' Melanie whispers.

I cover my nose with my hand and lean in to hear Melanie tell me that the woman in front of the classroom is Mrs Ho. She's standing in for Miss Morape, who's on a course to learn how to teach and won't be coming to school for the next two weeks. Miss Morape is definitely my kind of teacher. I miss her already.

Mrs Ho has the face of one of those babushka dolls. Her eyes are like tadpoles. They flash and gleam like a fanatic as she tells us to take out our Shakespeares – we're studying *Romeo and Juliet* this term. I think not.

I carry on reading *Twilight*. I got it from the library yesterday and I can't put it down. I read until midnight last night, then Fluffy came in and said, 'Lights out, it's your first day at your new school tomorrow. If you don't get eight hours' sleep you won't be able to perform to your potential.'

I read for another hour in the bathroom, wrapped up in my duvet in the bath. The cold water faucet is faulty and water dripped on to my feet. I didn't notice. I didn't even notice when Fluffy banged on the door and said, 'Please, April. Please, stop hogging the bathroom. Stop reading that book. You're an addict.'

My name is April-May and I am addicted to Twilight.
Hello, April-May.

I tried to resist this book when it made the bestseller list, but I have succumbed like a billion other teenagers all over the world. I am an addict.

Welcome to Stephenie Meyers Anonymous, April-May.

I need help. I need to get my hands on New Moon *as soon as I'm done with* Twilight. *I need to feed my addiction.*

I read *Twilight* as the class reads *Romeo and Juliet*. Time passes and I do not notice Mrs Ho writing on the board. I do not hear her walking up and down between the desks as the schloeps write notes in their books and she reads Shakespeare.

Edward the vampire is leaning towards Bella and I'm

just aching for that icy kiss. I lift my face as I sense his cold lips approach mine. I close my eyes. 'Kiss me, Edward,' I whisper. But when I open my eyes all I see is Mrs Ho.

Cold Fact No. 1

It is illegal in some countries to call your kids stupid names. Like you can't call your kid '4Real' in New Zealand, or 'Brfxxccxxmnpccccllllmmnprxvclmnckssqlbb11116' in Sweden, or even 'Prince' in the Netherlands.

Two

Fluffy's home by the time I get back from Melanie's house. He's throwing two-minute noodles into a pot.

'Two minutes,' I tell him as he stares at the clock on the kitchen wall. 'You don't need to time them. They'll float to the top when they're done.'

He glances at the clock one last time and then asks me where the heck I've been.

I tell him I've been smoking weed with the bad boys at school. Then I see his face and tell him, 'Jokes, Fluffy, jokes.'

Fluffy doesn't think I'm funny. He used to, but since Mom and him split the lounge suite and parted company he's been suffering from a serious sense-of-humour bypass.

'April, where *have* you been? I've been worried.'

Fluffy calls me April these days. Mom calls me May. When they're in the same room together (rarely) and speak to me at the same time, I feel schizoid tendencies coming on. Am I Autumn or am I Winter?

Fluffy pokes the noodles with his finger and looks even more worried when they start sinking.

I tell Fluffy I've been at the mall with Melanie, buying a new navy-blue school bag and some navy-blue socks. I nickies my fingers because I've been at the movies seeing *Twilight*, which between me and you is the last time I'll ever go to the movies with big-mouth Melanie.

She's seen *Twilight* seven times. She knows the dialogue off by heart and spoke the lines throughout the show. Loudly.

'Keep your mouth shut, Melly,' I told her.

She said she couldn't breathe.

It took all my self-control to stop myself from sinking my teeth into her neck.

Afterwards we hung out at her house. House? The place is a mansion. Two storeys with a swimming pool, a tennis court and a koi pond, all enclosed by an electric fence with an armed guard at a gatehouse.

I read Melly's copy of *Twilight* while she typed up my punishment essay on *Romeo and Juliet* with two fingers.

When she was done, I let her cover my school books in brown paper and plastic until it got dark and her mom said, 'Don't you have a home to go to?'

She looks just like Melly but she breathes through her nose.

Melly refused to let me borrow her copy of *Twilight*. She's learning it off by heart. She says she's going to know every one of the books like the back of her hand.

Fluffy looks relieved to hear I spent the afternoon with Melly and mashes the top of his head so his hair gets all fluffy, like a ball of black wool that's become so tangled that you need a thin-toothed comb to tease it apart.

Let me tell you about Fluffy. He's thirty-five years old and he's a blinking vulture. That's what some people call people in Fluffy's line of work. Fluffy drives a tow-away vehicle for Willie's Wreckers. He's the guy at the scene of the accident who jacks your car before the ambulance arrives (and then hits you with the bill before you can get buried).

Fluffy has this nifty little two-way radio, which is tapped into the police frequency. He has it on day and night. He's the guy who smiles when he hears the words 'pile-up on the freeway'. Then he's off like a rocket.

Fluffy hasn't always been a blinking vulture. Three months ago he was a bloody vampire. He sucked the blood out of the lives of innocent people and turned them into monsters. That's how Mom describes Fluffy's previous line of work. 'Journalists! Bloody vampires! What's the difference?' she says.

Mom can be cruel. As cruel as the bosses at the East Rand knock-and-drop newspaper who got bitten in the neck by the recession and had to downsize, rationalise, tighten their belts and retrench Fluffy last year.

Driving a tow truck is a way to pay the bills, apparently. A stopgap until Fluffy can get back into journalism or publish his best-selling novel. Then we'll move to Hollywood to sell the film rights and become slumdog millionaires.

Until then we're slumming it at Chez Matchbox, a house the size of Melly's en-suite bathroom. It gives me and Fluffy an uber-cosy space to lay our heads for as long as he can keep paying the mortgage.

The best thing about Chez Matchbox is the back garden. It's big enough to swing a dog and is shaded by an old sour-sour tree (*Eugenia myrtifolia*). The berries are as pink and sour as Fluffy's face when he reads his bank statements every month.

'How was your first day at your new school?' Fluffy asks me. His whole forehead collapses into a zillion lines when he asks this. I see his gloomy forehead and I flash back to Mrs Ho at my shoulder eight hours before.

'This is not Shakespeare,' she said.

Perceptive. No idiot, is our Mrs Ho. 'This is Stephenie Meyer,' I told her.

She picked *Twilight* off my desk and held it in the air like it was a snotty tissue. 'Trash,' she said.

'*Twilight*,' I told her.

14

She walked to the front of the class with my *Twilight* and gave us all a fifteen-minute lecture about good literature. Good literature is: Austen, Brontë, C. S. Lewis. She started ticking off her alphabet of acceptable authors. She faltered at D, so I helped her out with Dostoyevsky. I even spelt it for her. And gave her his first name: Fyodor.

Just for that she confiscated *Twilight* for two weeks and I got a five-hundred-word punishment essay on *Romeo and Juliet*. She evidently despises Russian writers.

I tell Fluffy that my first day at my new school was good.

He shakes his head and says, 'Good, good, good.' It's so important that this school works out, he continues. I must do good this term. I must perform to my potential.

He says this at least once a day, so I find myself saying it as he says it, just like Melly in the movie.

Fluffy says there's no need for you to get lippy with me, young lady. This is serious. I can't keep you if you don't do good. 'I'll have to give you back to your mother.'

I say this for him before he gets there. He laughs and says I'm impossible. He then looks despondent again because he wants to do everything possible to keep me.

Me getting a bursary to Trinity College is a big deal for Fluffy. It's a good school. Not like the rubbish one I went to last year. If I don't do good this term I'll get skopped back to the old school and have to live with Mom in Pretoria.

Fluffy asks about my teachers. I tell him about Finger. This makes Fluffy happy. His eyes light up. Fodder for his novel (he's still only on chapter one).

I tell him that Mr Goosen's finger got bitten off by a mad dog called Neville when he was trying to stop him from savaging a pair of newborn twins in their pram. When the paramedics arrived they couldn't find Mr Goosen's finger and Neville had to be chopped in half without anaesthetic, right there on the street. They found the top of Mr Goosen's finger in a digested mess of dog food and other strange-looking goop, but it was too late to sew it back on.

Fluffy loves this story. He takes notes and asks lots of questions. I must remember to ask Melly how it really happened.

I don't tell Fluffy about Mrs Ho. Punishment essays always make him dismal. It's not a good start, April. It's not a good start at your new good school. I can almost hear him say it.

We try and eat our overcooked ten-minute noodles and Fluffy drinks a couple of non-alcoholic beers. Fluffy's never been a big boozer, but he's on the wagon these days as he can never predict when there's going to be a pile-up on the N1 to Pretoria. He's got to be sharp when it happens.

It happens just as Fluffy's scraping the noodles into an

old ice-cream tub and he flies off like a vulture to feast on the misfortune of reckless drivers.

I spend the rest of the evening pining for the last three chapters of *Twilight* – the ones I never got to read at Melly's house. I make do with *Romeo and Juliet*. Totally wet. And I know from my reading of History that in Elizabethan times most of them had lost their teeth before they were old enough to kiss.

I want to talk to Mom. I want to tell her about the first day at my new good school. I want to tell her about how Mr Goosen lost his finger in a brutal hijacking. How it was blown clean off his hand as he pushed the bad guy's gun away from his temple. But Mom and me can't connect. Fluffy says he'll only be able to buy me a cellphone when Oxford Road collapses on to the Gautrain at rush hour.

I cover the seeping blisters on my ankles with bits of toilet paper and sticky tape and try not to think about Mom. Instead I think about Edward the vampire and Bella and toothless Romeo pining for his dead Juliet.

The bits of sticky tape come loose and my blisters chafe against my duvet. I think of Mrs Ho. I wonder where I can find an apothecary to buy some poison.

Cold Fact No. 2

In times of recession, some economists use the Noodle Index. The more instant noodles people eat, the worse the state of the economy of a country. But in both good and bad years, more noodles are eaten in Chinese households than in any other country.

Three

Fluffy looks worried. He checks the clock on the kitchen wall and says we're running late. Really late. His two-way radio is screaming blood and guts on the table and he says, 'April, we really, really must get the show on the road.'

I tell him that I feel the onset of Cat Scratch Disease. I really, really can't go to school. I need to take a sickie.

Cat Scratch Disease (CSD) is a fantastic illness which is hard to diagnose. It's caused by bacteria carried in cat saliva (*Bartonella henselae*) and it gives you flu-like symptoms and makes your lymph glands swell up. I've had it at least three times and we don't even have a cat.

Fluffy says, 'Oh no, not again. I'm not calling her. Please, April, it's over. Please, we have to move on.'

Fluffy's in a tizz and he's rubbing his hair all over the place. He thinks I'm pulling the same stunt I pulled last year when Fluffy and Mom were first living apart. I had

21

several rare and hard-to-diagnose diseases eleven times (sleeping sickness, tummy ache, broken-heart pain) and every time Mom had to call Fluffy to come round to the house.

I finally figured out that there was just no way they'd get back together again and allowed them to get divorced. But bad habits are hard to break.

Fluffy sits on my bed. 'I love you more than anything else in the whole wide world, April. The whole wide world. And your mother loves you too.' (More than anything else in the whole wide world.)

'You just don't love each other.'

Fluffy sighs. 'We loved each other. We made you.'

Fluffy and me have never had 'that talk'. What he doesn't know is that I know that love often has very little to do with making babies – even praying mantises do it and then the lady bug bites the poor man mantis's head off.

Fluffy sees the doubt on my face and insists that he really, really did love my mother. I don't ask him how on earth he could have stopped, then. And what's it going to take for him to stop loving me. I don't want to give him any ideas so I leap out of bed and tell him that all of a sudden I'm feeling fine.

I play Russian roulette with Fluffy's thesaurus and open it randomly: P. My word for the day is 'protean'. I have to use similes for protean five times today. I tell Fluffy that the killer Cat Scratch Disease can be erratic (protean), and that I really am in fine fettle again.

Fluffy drops me outside the school gates and drives off to his favourite spot, on a sharp bend near the highway where people in a rush to work ten-to-one wipe out. When it's raining he says it's five-to-one. There's a lot more job satisfaction in the summer when it pours.

I think about going to school and performing to my potential. I look down at my bare legs and wonder if the bits of toilet paper and sticky tape will hold up against my school shoes for another day. I think about my *Romeo and Juliet* punishment essay, which I forgot next to my breakfast of burnt toast.

'Crispy, not burnt,' Fluffy insisted.

'You can eat it then,' I told him.

I wait for Fluffy's tow truck to turn the corner and then I head for the 7-Eleven on the corner. I buy a packet of Texan Plain cigarettes and a carton of full-cream milk. I never buy the flavoured milks. They're so unhealthy.

I make for the park across the road. As parks in Jozi go it's pretty standard: obligatory plastic bags snagged on palisade fence; mass planting of weeds in borders; pockets of ciggie box-sized grass for picnics; trampoline, see-saw and car tyre swings – set on concrete to maximise impact during a fall. And one or two plane trees that managed to get away.

It starts to rain. The weather can be so changeable

(protean). I say thanks to the gods for smiling so beam-
ishly on Fluffy today. I also say no thanks to a kind old
tramp man next to the see-saw who says I can share his
blanket and his bottle of something smelly and fermented.

I sprint for a large plane tree near the swings and wait
until the first shower subsides. It stops raining and I drink
my milk. The vitamins A, D and K pour down my throat
with a dollop of calcium and I say hamba-suka to osteo-
porosis as I feel my teeth grow and strengthen.

'Milk's good for the bones.'

I stop drinking. You can't drink and talk to yourself at
the same time now, can you?

'It makes them strong. And it's good for the teeth.'

I look up and I see *Twilight*. I see Edward the vampire.

He's swaying backward and forward on the swing and
he's looking at me with his pale eyes. Eyes like lime juice.
He's smoking a cigarette. The smoke pours out of his nose
like the smoke out of the exhaust pipe on Fluffy's tow truck.

I give Edward the vampire my carton of milk and he
flicks his cigarette on to the ground. He grinds it out with
his bare foot.

He drinks some milk and hands the carton back to me.
My heartbeat is erratic (protean). He offers me a cigarette;
Camel soft pack. I take one. I don't know why. Everyone
with half a brain knows that smoking makes you sick and
gives you smelly breath.

If Finger were here he'd be giving me a History lesson on the evils of smoking. Perhaps not. I checked out that four-fingered hand yesterday. The sides of his fingers were the colour of old mustard. And he smelt like all the desperados who hang outside the malls feeding their addictions in their work breaks.

Smoking's not my gift, but I try and perform to my potential. I lean forward as Edward the vampire lights my Camel. I wonder if he can smell my blood. Is he thirsting for it? I smell singed hair and draw back quickly before the flame cremates the other half of my eyebrow. He snatches my cigarette impatiently, lights it, and then gives it back.

His name is not Edward. It's Sebastian. I tell him I'm Bella. He shows me how to drag the smoke into my mouth, slowly into my lungs and then out into a stream of smoke rings. When I cough he donders me on my back and says I'll get it, just practise. I hope I get it before I expire from throat rot.

He's evidently been practising lots because he clicks his jaw like a mechanical robot out of the sci-fi movies and only coughs between puffs.

'You're bunking school, Bella,' he says. And smiles. His teeth aren't sharp. They're white and blunt and he has a large gap in the front.

'So are you, Bas.' My mouth tastes disgusting so I flick

the cigarette on to the ground and I watch him do that thing with his bare feet.

'I'm sick. I have pneumonia.' He shows me his sick note. It says that he's been booked off school for three days.

Sebastian and I hang out for a while. He tells me he lives in one of the big houses across the road from the school. Rich kid. His mother and father are both doctors. Very rich.

I tell him I've got a teacher on my back called Mrs Ho who's causing me grief. Sebastian pulls a face like he knows the creature. He says his father is a diabetes specialist. He can kill someone by injecting insulin between their toes. And no one would ever be able to suss it. Interesting.

His cellphone rings and he takes the call. Sebastian tells his mother that he's getting some rest and keeping warm in bed. He reminds her to bring home seasons one and two of *Lost* and some apple juice. And his new golf clubs. And Kentucky.

It starts to rain again (Go Fluffy!) and Sebastian says he'll check me around. If I give him my cell number maybe he'll call me. Maybe.

I tell him my cellphone fell in the jacuzzi and I hold nickies behind my back.

He thinks I'm playing hard to get. He looks interested.

He says he'll defs check me around. I hope so with all my bleeding heart.

Sebastian tosses his Nike takkies into his backpack and says he's going home to surf the net. I don't want to even start thinking about how much I want a computer, and a wireless connection.

I jump around on the trampoline for a couple of hours and make the tramp man balance me out on the see-saw until he refuses to play any more and hides under his blanket. He won't come out even when I offer to share my polony rolls.

It's pouring buckets and I think I need to surf home before I drown. I'm sprinting across the road when a car hoots and skids to a stop. Pedestrian accidents aren't a big thing in Fluffy's business model otherwise I'd be throwing myself in front of cars all day to improve our cash flow.

The car pulls over to the side of the road as the cars behind it hoot and flash their lights. A woman gets out of the car, pulling an umbrella behind her. She opens it with some difficulty.

'You. Girl. Where are you going?' A cross face stares at me from under the dripping umbrella.

Oh no. It's Mrs Ho.

Cold Fact No. 3

A broken heart is a metaphor used to describe intense emotional pain after losing a loved one, through death, divorce, break-up, moving, being rejected or other means. There is also a condition known as Broken Heart Syndrome – where a traumatising incident triggers the brain to distribute chemicals that weaken heart tissue. Some elephants in Africa have been known to die from Broken Heart Syndrome. The symptoms of a broken heart are tightness of the chest, loss of appetite, insomnia, anger, nostalgia, apathy, et cetera.

Four

Mrs Ho drags me through the quad of jeering kids, waiting for their rides home. *Busted! Busted! Busted! You are so busted!* They snigger as she hauls me dripping into her classroom.

I see Melly breathing heavily at the end of the corridor. She waggles her hand at me, wishing me good luck.

Mrs Ho props her umbrella by the door and makes like Fluffy when he peels an onion: off with the raincoat, then the jacket, then the wellies. She emerges like a slimline matryoshka doll out of her various layers of protective clothing, ready for action.

I'm now standing barefoot in Mrs Ho's classroom. She's stuffing my shoes with newspaper. 'You can't walk around without socks,' she says, handing me a navy-blue pair out of the Lost Property Box. 'You can use these, April-May.'

Like use them for draining pasta? They're like crocheted doilies, covered in holes.

Mrs Ho rummages through the Lost Property Box and gives me a navy-blue satchel. It's manky with the remains of spilt yoghurt and squashed banana. 'This is the regulation satchel. It needs a wash, but it will do, April-May.'

Do what? Infect me with botulism?

I look at the dirty satchel and the socks and then I look at Mrs Ho. I look at the bits of toilet paper and sticky tape dripping off the backs of my ankles and I put the socks on.

Mrs Ho watches me with those tadpole eyes swimming crazily around after a bit of algae in her babushka face.

'You are new at this school.' She's not asking me, she's telling me. She has my file open on her lap and she's reading it. Her legs are crossed at her ankles and her eyes are crossing the page as she speed-reads my history. 'You are on an academic bursary, April-May. The lucky one out of the two hundred and sixty who applied.'

I am indeed. I feel very lucky.

'Your father works in Disaster Management?'

He does. It's true. I filled out the forms myself. 'He's in the automobile industry,' I say. I don't want to go into all the gory details: children without safety belts with their heads through windscreens; firemen with mechanical wrenches trying to pry body parts from behind steering wheels; Fluffy throwing up by the side of the road as he waits to extract his pound of flesh and tow away a car that will never see the highway again.

'The automobile industry?'

She's not going to let it go. So I go for it. I tell her about the time Fluffy roared up to the scene of an accident. It was two taxis on their way back to Zimbabwe. The luggage was piled high to the heavens and the passengers were packed in like baked beans into a hot potato. The one taxi's rear-view mirror was missing and the driver didn't see the other taxi trying to overtake; trying to make it to the border before it closed so that his passengers wouldn't have to sleep by the side of the road until the next day.

'There were twenty-two of them in the final body count. Thirteen children and nine adults laid out by the side of the road when Fluffy arrived. Except, of course they weren't sleeping. Not like Juliet,' I say, including a literary touch.

Mrs Ho looks like she wants to upchuck into my new-old navy-blue school bag. Her face is a green swamp and her tadpole eyes are drowning in the detritus. 'Your father drives a tow truck?'

My ears are blocked with water but I'm sure she says 'blinking vulture' under her breath.

Who's a blinking vulture? It's an honest job. It's not like Fluffy's a lawyer or a teacher. He works for a living.

I give Mrs Ho one of the Willie's Wreckers business cards that I keep in my blazer, in case she's ever involved in a smash-up. I'm their unofficial PR. She takes the card and puts it in her pocket. Her hand is shaking. I see the signs of post-traumatic stress. I want to tell her to put her head between her legs and breathe like Melly – out through her mouth in rapid gasps.

Then Mrs Ho gets her groove back and flicks her head like she's got whiplash. 'I think I've heard quite enough, April-May,' she says, getting ugly and demanding to see my punishment essay on *Romeo and Juliet*.

I flash back to the burnt toast. The essay lying next to it. Fluffy wrapping the toast in a piece of foolscap paper with some leftover noodles and shoving it into his lunch box for the road. My essay.

Mrs Ho sees she's got me reversing in fifth gear and she goes in for the kill. She says my failure to perform (to my potential) means I've got another punishment essay to do. Her eyes light up and I can see she wants to be too clever.

She wants a five-hundred-word essay on the differences and similarities between two great literary works: *Romeo and Juliet* and *Twilight*. She says the name of my library book with a mean grin. She thinks she has me.

What she forgets is that I'm the one who got the bursary out of two hundred and sixty applicants. I'm the lucky one. The one who got to come to this good school. She may be clever, but I'm now performing to my potential.

'I need to finish the book.'

'*Romeo and Juliet?*' She says it with a sneer. Like she thinks she knows me. Like I'm one of those kids who can't read books written by a funny old man in knickerbockers and stockings and crack a bursary.

But I finished *Romeo and Juliet* last night. It's my *Twilight* I'm aching for. I see Sebastian's face in the park as he blows cigarette smoke into my face. Passive smoking isn't one of my guilty pleasures so I turn away. I want Edward the vampire.

Mrs Ho gets Stephenie Meyer out of the dark desk drawer where she's been suffocating and gives her to me. I grab her and page to the back of the book, to the last three chapters, and start reading.

Mrs Ho tells me I can spend the afternoon in detention doing the essay. She'll be back to check on me. I don't notice her leaving and shutting the door behind her. I'm with Edward the vampire and Bella. I cannot be disturbed. Except by Melly, who's outside in the corridor, fugging up the window.

I leave her breathing hard for a while, until I've finished the book, then I let her in. She throws herself at me and ventilates the back of her neck. She is just so sorry. So sorry. She has a present for me to make me feel better.

I am just so glad. So glad. It's *New Moon*. And it's not a library book. It's brand new. I sniff the pages. They smell of clean paper and Edward's blood.

'You bought this for me?'

Melly says she did.

I don't respond, but I decide that Melly is the best friend any breathing person could ever have. And as a 'thank you' I allow her to write my essay as I start to read *New Moon*. I slap her fingers when she dots her 'i's with pizzas. And when she adds porcine tummies to her 'g's and spaghetti tails to her 'l's.

I tell Melly that her spelling reads like an idiot's guide to texting. Melly says texting is for yesterday's idiots. She Twitters. I tell Melly to read *New Moon* out loud to me instead while I twitter away at the essay – just in time for Mrs Ho's arrival.

Mrs Ho shoos Melly out of the classroom and gives me a long lecture about how I certainly haven't brought the house down with my performance these past two days. How she's watching me. That as a bursary kid I need to – and then she says it just like Fluffy – perform to my potential. If I don't, I'll be out of Trinity College faster than she can say, 'Do you want a lift home?'

I look up from my essay and give her a blank stare.

'Can I give you a lift home?' Mrs Ho asks.

It's pouring down. I calculate the odds of arriving home alive in a taxi. Then I calculate the odds in Mrs Ho's Toyota Corolla. I take the lift.

On our way home Mrs Ho asks me questions. Can't she see? I'm trying to read.

But Mrs Ho is persistent. Her nose quivers like a starved rat after a bit of bacon. She inquires about my 'family arrangement' (divorced). About my mother (living in Pretoria). About Fluffy (roaring off after a high-impact collision, hopefully). I feel like I'm on *Oprah* but I don't cry or jump on the car seat. I keep my answers brief. Finally she asks me what my favourite subject is and I tell her that my interests are variable (protean), but that mostly I like English. She says, 'Oh, yes.' And I go back to reading *New Moon*.

Mrs Ho pulls up at a traffic light and looks over at me. She may give my father a buzz, she says. She says it very quietly to see if I'm really reading, or listening. Doesn't she know us bursary kids can walk and chew gum at the same time? I pretend I don't hear her. I don't tell her about Fluffy's disconnected status. She can call him at Willie's Wreckers where the switchboard goes straight to the answer message.

Three minutes later we pull up in front of Chez Matchbox. I tell Mrs Ho that I'd invite her in, but I can see she's busy. I can also see Fluffy busy with his head under the bonnet of his tow truck.

Mrs Ho sees the tow truck and that bushy tangle of black hair bobbing away as Fluffy waves the spanner around. I admit it's a pretty horrible sight, but Mrs Ho's face is chalk white – it's like she's seen a bloody vampire. It's all I can do to get out of the car before she screeches off, leaving me standing on the pavement without as much as a 'don't forget to finish your essay and make sure you're at school tomorrow'.

Cold Fact No. 4

In an average lifetime, people spend four years travelling in cars and six months waiting for red lights to turn green.

Five

Fluffy puts his tools away, cleans up and joins me in the kitchen over a cup of rooibos tea. He leans his elbows on the table, his facial expressions fluctuating (protean): Despair-relief. Despair-hopelessness. Despair-relief.

'I've been fired,' he finally says. And then he laughs like a maniac.

I take the box of Texan Plains out of my blazer pocket and place it gently on the table. Fluffy doesn't smoke unless it's an emergency. This is one of those.

Fluffy snatches up the fags. His expression now says: where did you get the cash? 'Your taxi fare?' he asks, looking glad and guilty at the same time.

I tell him that I got a lift home with my favourite teacher, Mrs Ho, and had spare cash to spread around on essentials.

Fluffy waits for me to give the go-ahead. I decide when it's an emergency. I determine when Fluffy gets to smoke.

And I buy the product. This is our way of trying to get him to crack his addiction.

Eventually I get the matches and he lights up.

'They say I'm too thin,' he says after a couple of puffs. 'They fired me.' He laughs again and tries to spit a bit of tobacco off the top of his lip.

I reach for my emergency stash of ZOO biscuits and start scraping the white zebra off the pink icing while Fluffy smokes. I see my cellphone disappearing down the hole in Oxford Road. I see myself recycling the rooibos tea bags on the washing line until Fluffy finds another job. I sentence cold-blooded Willie from Willie's Wreckers to a smash-up on Joe Slovo Drive.

'They weighed me at lunchtime and said I was three kilos below my goal weight. I was causing bad morale among the fatties. They've had to let me go.'

I snatch the box of Texan Plains off the table. Fraud! Con artist! Schemer! Swindler! Deceiver! Crook! 'You got fired from Weigh-Less?'

Fluffy nods, and then he grins at me.

I put the ZOO biscuits away. Emergency over.

Fluffy enrolled at Weigh-Less at the beginning of the year. It came free with his medical aid, something the newspaper allowed him to keep for six months when they cut costs and cut him loose.

It was Fluffy's attempt at moving on. His pal Ishmael

at Willie's Wreckers said Weigh-Less was the best way to meet the ladies – the chubby ones trying to get thin would be up for it. With Mom gone, he had to get a life.

For the next three weeks Fluffy brought back recipes and booklets and tips on how to keep the weight off (eight glasses of water a day), but he didn't bring home a tubby. I was glad. And I could see that Fluffy was kind of relieved too. He's not ready to get a life like Mom.

Mom's been seeing a guy called Sarel. He's a hotshot attorney at a big law firm in Waterkloof, a posh suburb in Pretoria. 'From one bloody vampire to the next without even taking a breath.' That's what Fluffy says about Mom and Sarel. It makes me see blood too.

Fluffy makes sad eyes at me but I refuse to give him another cigarette to compensate for losing out on large love, and ask him if he's ever going to cook supper.

'Fish and chips,' Fluffy tells me. Ishmael is bringing takeaways to celebrate the day's carnage.

Ishmael arrives with three lots of fish and chips in newspaper. He desperately needs to take Fluffy's place at Weigh-Less. His meaty rolls fall over the belt of his trousers and he sweats like processed cheese in cling wrap when he exerts himself. Like now, as he rips open the newspaper and divvies up the fish and chips. He also needs to get his eyes checked, because half the chips land up on his plate.

43

Ishmael says he's concerned about Fluffy. Willie from Willie's Wreckers says Fluffy's a bleeding dove. Fluffy stares miserably at his fish and pushes it around the plate. Ishmael's beating up on him like he's a stray dog caught rummaging in the trash: Fluffy's letting the side down. He's a disgrace to the profession. He's got custard in his spinal cord. If he doesn't pull up his socks he's going to get the sack. Willie has him in his sights.

Ishmael tells me that Fluffy's been undercharging for his services. Undercharging as in: 'Don't worry, I'll tow away your totalled car and meet you at the hospital. You can pay me after you've switched off your wife's life support and paid all the medical bills.'

Ishmael says Fluffy needs a competitive edge. He needs to become hard-core like him and the other wreckers. He needs to do something about his situation, fast. Ishmael and Fluffy look to the bursary kid for some ideas.

I tell Ishmael the first thing that needs to happen is for Fluffy to remove the *How am I driving? Phone 082 346 4532* sign from the back of his tow truck. It doesn't inspire confidence among the customers. And Fluffy must stop driving like a snail in the fast lane just because he's scared of also becoming a customer of Willie's Wreckers. He needs to speed up. Cut to the chase.

Ishmael's taking Fluffy's plight on board. He feels responsible. It was he, after all, who got Fluffy involved

44

in the business when Fluffy got culled from his newspaper job. They go back a long way. Right to the first month of Fluffy's cub reporting days on the newspaper, when he was on the graveyard shift chasing ambulances.

Ishmael was Fluffy's first source; his deep throat from the day they met outside a shopping centre, half of which had collapsed on to a parking lot – Fluffy's big scoop.

Fluffy and Ishmael crack open a couple of non-alcoholic beers and start strategising over some work performance tips for Fluffy while I get on with finishing my essay.

I employ one of Fluffy's newspaper techniques. The headline is the most important thing. You have to get the reader's attention. I cross out: *The similarities and differences between* Romeo and Juliet *and* Twilight. And replace it with: *Blood and guts in an ill-fated love triangle*.

I divide the text of the essay using smaller headlines. These include: *Bella commits fashion crimes* (her clothes are rags compared to Juliet's cutting-edge couture); *Romeo at a loss for words* (his inability to speak decent English like Edward the vampire is tragic) and *Juliet grounded for life*. I'm just about to elaborate on the tragedy of Juliet not being a child from a broken home like Bella (where parental guidance is less strict and you can score with inappropriate boys without too much aggro) when Fluffy says the lady across the road wants to see me. I have a phone call.

Mrs Barnard runs a telephone booth on the pavement across the road from our house. She managed to jemmy her landline a year or so back and charges a few rand to all those people in the street who are deficient in the connection stakes: those who don't have landlines, cellphones, Berries or Internet access. Like Fluffy and me.

Mom's on the phone. She's hysterical. She says she's just received a telephone call from Miss Show.

'Mrs Ho?' The line is bad.

Mom says, whatever you blinking want to call her, she's a teacher from Trinity College. She called her to say that I had bunked school and had already had detention on the second day and that things are going to the dogs with my bursary.

I tell Mom that Mrs Ho is a psychoneurotic.

Mom says, 'What? What did you say, May?'

I say, 'Mrs Ho's a basket case.' She's disturbed, unwired and compulsively uptight. A bit like Mom.

'That may well be, May,' Mom replies, 'but I'm coming round over the weekend to thrash things out with your father.' And to thrash me to an inch of my life if she finds out I've been acting silly buggers at school. Apparently Mrs Ho's coming too, so Mom's bringing Sarel for moral support.

I tell her to drive safe. The road from Pretoria to Jozi is prime fender-bender real estate on holidays and weekends.

I go back inside and tell Fluffy that Mom's visiting over the weekend. Saturday to be precise. His face lights up.

I tell Fluffy that Mom's bringing Sarel as back-up. Fluffy's face goes very red and he mangles his hair. He wants to know why Mom's coming on Saturday. It's not her weekend to see me. She's only supposed to do me twice a month.

I tell Fluffy she wants to discuss matters of an educational nature. My pet teacher, Mrs Ho, will be joining us to discuss my future.

Fluffy looks proud. He tells Ishmael for the third time about my bursary to the good school. The bursary that keeps me in Jozi and away from Mom and the rubbish school in Pretoria.

I leave them chatting and retrieve my other punishment essay out of Fluffy's lunch box. I excavate the pages from the remains of the burnt toast and noodles. It's as good as new.

I spend the evening washing half a dozen pairs of Fluffy's navy-blue socks. The ones Mrs Ho gave me have all but unravelled, and I try and stretch Fluffy's socks between two chairs to grow them to my leg length.

I imagine going back in time from the twenty-first century, past Shakespeare, all the way back to medieval times when stretching was in vogue.

I picture Mrs Ho stretched out on a rack. Her joints

crack and her tendons snap and she loses her vocal cords as she screams for mercy.

But I am pitiless. I am relentless. This is a dog-eat-dog world. By ratting on me to Mom and threatening to visit my home, Mrs Ho has crossed the line.

I fall asleep making plans of how to stop Mrs Ho's invasion. She's in for a big shock.

Cold Fact No. 5

India has more cellphones than toilets. There is approximately one cellphone for every person in India. The ratio of toilets to cellphones at Chez Matchbox is 1:0.

Six

The first shock of the day happens in my Biology class.

Call me Fickle. Call me Whimsical. Call me Capricious. But when it comes to a toss-up between Biology and English, I blow hot and cold.

Biology, or Natural Science as they call it at Trinity College, is my favourite subject next to English. Sometimes they're so close I can't choose.

I have two sets of books next to my bed – literary works like *Twilight* (and, since last night, *New Moon*) and the great books concerning the study of life. Biology.

Fluffy says my brain can't come to an agreement between its two parts as to which should rule. My right brain, which loves words and English, is at constant odds with my left brain, which favours logic.

Mom says there's no argument about it: May is going to be a doctor, she's a left-brain kind of girl. Fluffy says, for the sake of bickering, April is going to be a great writer, like he was before he went into the wrecking business. They nit and pick about it all the time.

I think there's plenty of time to think about it later. For the time being, I'm happy to be whole-brained.

I'm sitting at the back of the class with Melly and she's telling me about this oxygen tank she's got to sleep with to help her breathe. She has sleep apnoea, which is a condition that causes her to stop breathing at night. Her hands and feet also go bright pink because of the lack of oxygen.

Melly's panting all over me when she tells me this, so it appears she likes to make full use of the daylight hours to compensate for her inability to inhale/exhale when the sun goes down. Five minutes later I get a big shock.

It is not Melly's medical disclosures that take my breath away. Although, as a novice in the study of gene theory, I'm fascinated by Melly's primary units of inheritance: her genome, her DNA. What shocks me is the arrival of the Biology teacher (she who will assist me in shedding light on which of Melly's parents is to blame for her sleep apnoea).

I'm so stunned that her arrival instantly interrupts the activity I'm engaged in, which is trying to extract some of Melly's blood with a blade from my sharpener so I can study it for clues in the lab later.

'What in heaven's name are you doing with that filthy

blade?' Mrs Ho says, leaping across the classroom quicker than you can say, 'Mad vampire in flight!' to where Melly is voluntarily donating her blood to medical science.

I see Mrs Ho and I think 'impediment', which is a synonym for what I'm hatching to put in the way of her visit to my house tomorrow. Obstacle, block, booby trap, hindrance, restraint. They're all good words for what I'm plotting.

Mrs Ho, Melly tells me, while she's away at the secretary's office getting Melly a plaster and some antiseptic cream, is not only substituting for the skills-deficient Miss Morape, she's also the full-time Biology teacher.

On her return, Mrs Ho embarks upon her own little biological experiment into the 'principle of impediment'. She makes a lab rat called April-May sit in front of the class while we discuss genetics versus the environment.

My environment – sitting at the back of the class with Melly – is an obstacle to me performing to my genetic abilities. For this, I'm going to sit solo right under Mrs Ho's eye for the rest of the term until I can demonstrate that my genetic predisposition towards excellence has triumphed over my inclination to cause trouble at the back of the class.

I am not alone for long. I'm joined by a clot of thoughts and ideas about how to stop Mrs Ho causing trouble in my domestic environment. These thoughts keep me company throughout the Biology lesson and all the way to the end of the school day. I hardly miss Melly at all. I may have two brains, but I can be single-minded in emergencies.

I hang around after school until I see Mrs Ho leave her classroom. Then I put Plan A into action. Plan A is a bit of a hoary old chestnut. It's easy-peasy for anyone who's been to a rubbish school, like me. It's a piece of cake for a bursary kid whose best subject, along with English and Biology, is Design and Technology.

I used Plan A a dozen times on Fluffy and Mom last year, when I wanted them to be alone for long periods of time in a confined space so that they could realise that they loved each other more than anything else in the whole wide world, along with me.

I go to Mrs Ho's classroom, take the classroom door key off its nail by the cupboard and turn it in the lock, so that it is set to lock mode. Most people – like Fluffy and Mom – don't even notice until they've shut the door behind them, and then it's too late.

After the tenth time I kept Mom and Fluffy trapped inside their room for a twenty-hour stretch, Mom sat me down and said it really, really was too late and we just had to move on. I then went on to Plan B: Cat Scratch Disease. It's always best to have a couple of plans bubbling away in the pot.

I put Mrs Ho's Plan B into action. Plan B is a result of my circumstances. Not everyone can be lucky enough to have a father in the automobile industry who keeps hundreds of spare car keys for those little emergencies. Like when the mother of three comes to reclaim her car from Willie's Wreckers so that she can transport her husband's new wheelchair home after his six-month stay in hospital. No keys? Fluffy always has something that will fit.

I take Mrs Ho's car keys off her desk and I replace them with an identical set of keys for a Toyota Corolla. I then put Mrs Ho's keys at the back of her desk drawer – along with the classroom door key. I may be bent on creating hell and hindrance, but I'm not a mean thief.

I hang around the school for a while, reading *New Moon*, until I see Mrs Ho go back to her classroom. The door is wide, wide open – just as I had left it.

It's late in the day, but Mrs Ho's one of those trouble-some teachers who involves herself in extra lessons for the slow kids, and extramurals for the fast ones. Those little extras to keep the kids usefully employed and out of the malls.

I go to her classroom and give her the kind of smile that the suck-ups sitting in front of the class always give her.

'Yes?' She's busy reading one of my essays. The survivor

from the two-minute noodle-jacking has been placed at the end of the desk so I assume it's the one on *Twilight* and *Romeo and Juliet*.

'I came to see if you received my essays? I put them on your desk.'

Mrs Ho has tears in her eyes. I can't tell if she's laughing or crying.

She looks at my legs. Fluffy's over-stretched socks have collapsed around my ankles. She points to the essay in front of her. 'Tragic,' she says.

I conclude that they are tears of sadness. I tell her I'll be on my way then and she says she's going to be working for a while. Please shut the door on your way out.

I leave the room, leaving the door a little ajar. Then I wait.

Finally I hear her sigh and her chair scrape back as she gets up and pulls the door closed behind her. Locked in.

On my way off the school premises I see the parking lot is empty except for one Toyota Corolla. The security guard is listening to his iPod at the far end of the school. All is well.

I spend the evening at Melly's house, playing with her oxygen tank. She lets me use it to blow up hundreds of balloons and we beat each other up a bit in a balloon fight.

She asks me if we're having a party. Are we celebrating something?

I tell her we are indeed. It's the weekend tomorrow and my mom's coming to visit. Melly asks if anyone else is coming round.

I imagine Mrs Ho locked in her classroom all night. I see her climbing out of the window and setting herself free after hours of shouting. I fancy she scrapes the backs of her ankles the same way mine got mutilated on the first day of school.

I envisage Mrs Ho's frustration as she fails to open her car with Fluffy's spare key. Hours later I see her finally making it home late on Saturday afternoon – carless, exhausted, soaked to the skin and too late to come round to my house to cause trouble with Mom and Fluffy.

'It's just the family. And Sarel,' I tell Melly.

Mrs Ho regrets that she is otherwise engaged.

Cold Fact No. 6

People are scared of lots of stuff. Some fear heights (acrophobia), some panic when they are confined to small spaces (claustrophobia), others don't like being stared at by ducks or when peanut butter sticks to the roof of their mouth. Some people even suffer from nomophobia – the fear of being out of cellphone contact.

Seven

Fluffy and me spend Saturday morning trying to make the house look decent. It's important that Mom sees we're coping; that Fluffy is providing for my needs.

Fluffy's face is the embodiment of torment. 'We need to put on a brave face, April. Let's pull together.'

I lose the toss and get to clean the bathroom while Fluffy takes on the kitchen. In between sweating over bits of Fluffy's epidermis (which have been deposited around the plughole) with the aid of his toothbrush, I chuck all the dirty clothes into a rubbish bag. Three large rubbish bags for Fluffy to take to the laundromat. It's been two weeks since the last visit.

Fluffy leaves all the dirty pots to soak and says he'll be back in two ticks. He's off to get some groceries. One of us is going to have to cook the lunch. He roars off, forgetting the three bags of dirty washing on the pavement.

My word for today is 'restraint'. I am going to spend

the day restraining myself from expressing my desires, especially my physical desire to rip Sarel's wig off his head and choke him with it. I am going to be the model of self-control, forbearance and self-denial.

Fluffy comes back from the shops with meat. He got it at the shop that sells lamb at 'Mad Max prices' and he thinks that it's a good idea if I cook a curry. He likes a good hot curry, one that cleans out the sinuses and makes him sweat.

While I chop chillies, Fluffy carries on cleaning the kitchen. I show no moderation in my deployment of the chillies. (Sarel likes his curries mild.)

Ten minutes later Fluffy takes a break from cleaning and tastes the curry. 'It's not hot enough,' he grumbles and proceeds to chop more chillies with a vengeful knife.

Mom and Sarel arrive just as Fluffy is finishing straightening out the bedrooms. It's a close call – all the junk on our bedroom floors gets shoved into the broom cupboard – but our house is shipshape.

Let me tell you about Mom. Her name is Glorette and she's a public relations consultant, which is the polite name for a 'blinking spin doctor' (Fluffy's name for what Mom does).

Mom brainwashes people into believing that when they don't have food to eat, they're on a healthy diet, waging war on obesity. That when sole breadwinners lose their jobs, they're taking well-deserved early retirement. And when hundreds of people die on the roads during the Easter Weekend, it's a triumph for road safety. She can always fiddle the stats to show that deaths are down from last year.

Mom works for a small PR company in Pretoria. It's her job to turn defeats into victories, tragedies into comedies. She's a troubleshooter for all the charlatans in this world who lie and cheat the public. This is Fluffy's version.

Mom hugs me hard and says that she loves me more than anything else in the whole wide world. Fluffy sniffs at Sarel, and Sarel shakes Fluffy's hand, which is covered in chilli juice. Sarel and I don't touch.

Let me tell you about Sarel. The most important thing you should know about the man is that he's my mom's boyfriend, her beau, her admirer, her significant other. All the words that describe Sarel's status in Mom's life sting the inside of my mouth like a swarm of wasps – Mom managed to move on and get a life faster than Fluffy could finish serving divorce papers.

The other significant thing about Sarel is that he wears a wig. Sarel's rug is a shade darker than what is left of his normal hair. I look at Fluffy's healthy tangle of wool and at Sarel's thatch of inanimate weave and I exercise some restraint by sitting on my hands.

Sarel drives a Mercedes-Benz. He says his Porsche is

in the double garage back in Pretoria. Show-off! I check an impulse to sneer, 'So what else did you get for Christmas?'

Sarel says he likes to display public modesty in his choice of wheels as he doesn't want to encourage hijackers.

The other car in Sarel's garage is Fluffy's Polo. The one Mom got to keep along with the television and the pot plants. And the cellphone, which is ringing in Mom's bag: 'Hello.'

'It's Miss Show,' Mom whispers a second or two later.

The cricket in my head starts to chirp. I imagine Mrs Ho falling off the roof of the school and breaking her back. I envisage her Toyota Corolla getting traded in for a motorised wheelchair.

I try to rein in my galloping conscience by making rooibos. 'She's not coming?' I ask as I switch on the kettle. My face is a panorama of regret, relief and guilt. How could I have overlooked Mrs Ho's cellphone in the classroom?

'No, she's going to be late,' Mom says. 'She's been trapped by circumstance and now she's somehow locked herself out of her car.'

Then Mom says that she and Fluffy need to have a 'conversation' – which is another word for an argument – about me before Miss Show shows up.

I take my rooibos to the other side of the kitchen and read *New Moon* in between stirring the curry.

Sarel picks his nose and wipes his eyes with the same hand that shook Fluffy's chilli-juiced fingers. Then he doubles up in agony and runs into the bathroom to wash out his eyes before they explode.

Mom continues with the 'conversation', trying to ignore the gross sounds of her significant other rinsing traces of chilli juice out of his nasal passages.

'May's looking thin. Are you feeding her?'

'May's looking tired. Is she getting her eight hours?'

'May's looking shabby. Are you buying her new clothes?'

Mom shoots questions at Fluffy like a trigger-happy mercenary in a dirty war as he runs and dodges and searches desperately for some ammo with which to return her fire. Fluffy grabs the box of Texan Plains off the table and lights up under Mom's spitting eyes.

Mom hates smokers. She is a reformed smoker herself, which is why she's uncompromising in her loathing for anything containing tobacco and anyone using the drug.

Fluffy's looking as rough as a grizzly bear's knees, so I leave the curry to burn and join their 'conversation'. I assure Mom that I eat all the time, but I'm thin because I'm genetically disposed to being scrawny, like Fluffy (and not like Sarel, who is as fat as a drunk tick in a Petri dish of Melly's blood). I look tired because I've been studying very hard to perform to my potential at my new good school and I'm shabby because Fluffy has taken all my

65

clothes to the laundromat – as he does three times a week to ensure that I am turned out like a ramp model every day. I hold three sets of nickies behind my back.

Fluffy goes a bit green and runs outside. He comes back shaking his head. 'They were on the pavement. You didn't . . . ?' He looks at me hopefully.

I tell Fluffy that they were on the pavement, where he left them, the last time I looked.

Mom says she saw a scruffy man running off with three bags of rubbish when she arrived. 'Is there a problem?' she asks.

Fluffy and I shake our heads. These things happen. There's no point crying over spilt milk, or three bags of laundry which have absconded with a happy tramp man who can't believe his luck and thinks it's his birthday.

Mom's phone rings again.

'And the AA won't come?' Mom doesn't have to tell me, but she does anyway. Miss Show can't get into her car and the AA won't come.

Fluffy's face lights up as he sees an escape hatch. He grabs the keys to his tow truck and the bag of spares he likes to use in emergencies. Mom says he must wait for Sarel, Miss Show may need a lawyer, but Sarel won't come out of the bathroom. He can't. He's managed to lock himself inside and he's stuck. Mom gives me a look which says, 'Oh, no, May, not that hoary old chestnut again.'

I'm sorry, but there are evidently limits to my self-control. I decide to cut my losses and make a fast getaway with Fluffy while Mom deals with the sobbing Sarel, who hates confined spaces. How was I to know? Mom's only told me like a million times.

I grab an umbrella and shout to Mom that she mustn't forget to stir the curry. Fluffy and me are off to rescue Mrs Ho.

Cold Fact No. 7

Chewing gum can keep you from crying when cutting onions.
Wearing goggles or a mask works too.

Eight

Melly and me are floating on a lilo in the middle of Melly's swimming pool. We have smothered our bodies in suncream.

Melly looks at my skin and says it's too late. Suncream is about as much use to me as a used earbud. I'm a mixed-race South African. I'm fighting a losing battle against my genetic inheritance. I'll never be as pasty and interesting as her and Bella (and Edward the vampire). I flip Melly into the water and paddle to the edge of the pool while she drowns.

We lie on some towels and absorb all the benefits provided by the hole in the ozone layer while I tell Melly all about yesterday when Fluffy and me rescued Mrs Ho.

We'd arrived at the school just as the fire engine was leaving. They'd packed away the harness and the ladder they'd intended to use to get Mrs Ho down from her classroom window (after the security guard couldn't find the spare key for the door). And the axe they had finally used to break down the classroom door when Mrs Ho had declared herself to be a member of Vertigos Anonymous.

Mrs Ho was pretty hysterical. Her pale doll face was streaked with smoke (from trying to send smoke signals before she discovered her cellphone hiding under a pile of books in the dawn hours of Saturday morning) and her eyes were slitty, slitty slits. Tadpole embryos.

She'd shown very little restraint when she had seen Fluffy and me. 'Blinking vulture,' she'd yelled at Fluffy. Then she'd caught sight of me and pulled herself towards herself.

Melly pulls my hand. She wants to know why Mrs Ho called Fluffy a blinking vulture. It was a strange thing to be calling your knight in shining armour, was it not? I tell Melly that Mrs Ho was unhinged by her experience. She acted ugly to poor old Fluffy for the rest of the day. Her lack of gratitude was a mystery.

Fluffy, in contrast, was calm and professional – the way Willie from Willie's Wreckers had trained him to be. As calm as the time a truckload full of sheep on their way to the abattoir upended itself on the R21 to OR Tambo airport and it was discovered that most of the culling had been achieved gratis on the tarmac. Fluffy didn't eat lamb for a month – out of choice.

I'd sped up to Mrs Ho's classroom while Fluffy had gone with her to her car. Taking the keys from the back of the drawer, where I'd hidden them (I don't let this little cat out of the bag to Melly) the day before, I'd joined them in the parking lot.

'I've tried that, I've tried that. It won't work. I've tried it a million times.' Mrs Ho had stamped her feet at Fluffy as he'd clicked the remote on her/Fluffy's emergency car key and tried the key in the door.

Fluffy had shaken his head in bewilderment and then rummaged through his bag of spare car keys until he'd found a couple of sets for Toyota Corollas. He'd given the bag to me to hold (Mrs Ho had refused – very weird behaviour) and while he'd tried the other keys in the lock I'd slipped Mrs Ho's set – and the classroom key – into it. The evidence of my crime was now buried in the rest of Fluffy's collection. I was as home and as dry as I could ever be as the rain poured down on the umbrella I held over Fluffy as he pored over his emergency spares.

Fluffy had, at last, called it a day. 'I'm sorry, but I'm going to have to tow you to the yard.'

Mrs Ho had glared at him. 'Oh no, you won't. I'm not having *that* again.'

Melly interrupts my telling. 'What did she mean by that?'

I tell Melly that Mrs Ho had refused to let Fluffy tow

her car. Mean. She probably knew there was a bill attached. Times are tough. People are always looking for handouts.

'No, the part where she said she wasn't "having *that* again"?'

I tell Melly to hold her horses. All will be revealed. And she should put some more cream on her exposed tummy because from my vantage point her skin is manifesting third degree sunburn.

Fluffy had given Mrs Ho one of his calm and professional looks. 'Let's be sensible,' he'd said, putting his hand on her shoulder. 'I'll tow the car and then you can come back to my place for a curry.'

Mrs Ho had looked like she'd rather starve to death than ever sit down and eat with Fluffy. ('Kinky behaviour,' says Melly. I agree. Psycho.) Then she'd swiped his hand off her shoulder like he was a cockroach smuggling swine flu into a crèche.

But Fluffy's not a quitter and he had tried again. He'd told Mrs Ho that Mom was at the house cooking curry and waiting for her to come round to talk about April's (May's) education – as arranged. And trying to spring Sarel from the bathroom where he'd mysteriously locked himself. Fluffy had grinned at me as he'd said this. 'That hoary old chestnut,' he'd muttered gleefully.

Mrs Ho's eyes had disappeared into her head and then reappeared like toxic green gherkins. She'd caught our conspiratorial exchange and was just about to say, 'That's just too much of a coincidence,' when I'd reached into Fluffy's bag and handed him Mrs Ho's car keys.

'They fitted. How creepy. That was lucky,' Melly says.

I agree. It was a narrow escape. As narrow as Sarel's breakout through the bathroom window after Mom had ripped out the burglar bars.

Fluffy, always the gentleman, had offered to follow Mrs Ho home in case of a malfunction along the way, but Mrs Ho had shaken her head. Fluffy had insisted: 'No charge, this one's on me. You seem to be in shock and you really, really shouldn't be driving.'

So we'd followed Mrs Ho all the way home – her weaving about the road like a juiced-up old drunk a million times over the limit.

'She was drunk! That's why she was acting so bugged out. Reveal all,' Melly insists, gulping for breath.

I turn over on to my tummy, so that Melly can't see my face. I don't want her to see the battle that's going on between my left and right brains. The tussle between what I know to be wrong but what I feel to be right in my fight for survival against Mrs Ho.

When we'd arrived at Mrs Ho's house – a small house in a street of much bigger houses – a kid on crutches had rushed as fast as a kid on crutches can rush to the gate. But as soon as he had seen Fluffy's tow truck he'd looked like a three-ton truck had snuffed out his father on the N3 to Durban – en route to a family holiday by the sea – and that the rep from Willie's Wreckers was arriving to tell him that his mother was now gone too.

Melly says I've just got to be kidding. What a coincidence. That's precisely what happened to Mrs Ho and her family last year. It was a terrible accident.

I tell Melly that I agree with her. It really was a day of uncanny coincidences.

I roll over and try and forget the expression on Mrs Ho's face when she'd told the kid she was alive and well. 'Really, look at me, not a scratch.' That she would never leave him. That she loved him more than anything else in the whole wide world.

Mrs Ho hadn't even thanked Fluffy. She'd shuffled her son indoors and shouted to us that she'd make an appointment to see Fluffy and Mom the following week to discuss April-May's future at Trinity College. Then she'd slammed the door shut.

When we'd got home, the curry was burnt and Sarel looked like he needed a session on Melly's oxygen tank. He was wheezing all over his Mercedes-Benz, which just wouldn't, wouldn't start.

Mom had fallen off the wagon big time and was smoking Fluffy's Texan Plains as she waited for his collection of spare keys to see if one of them would do the trick.

It was at this point that I could have whipped out Sarel's car keys and the bathroom key, which I'd hidden in Fluffy's collection of chillies, and come clean. I could have turned my back on my mission to block Mrs Ho's attempts to stick her nose in my life.

But the wrong part of my brain had kicked in and my right brain took over. There was no way Mrs Ho was going to send me back to my rubbish school in Pretoria. She could not be allowed to cause trouble between Fluffy and me.

I knew then how Edward the vampire felt. I was going to hell for what I had done anyway. There was no turning back.

I'd allowed Fluffy to mess around with his miserable collection of keys until he gave up and told Sarel he'd have to tow the Benz to Willie's yard. Mom and Sarel would have to take a taxi home to Pretoria.

Fluffy had handed Sarel a bill for his services and winked at me to share his relish at the fury on Sarel's face.

But I could only see the face of a boy on crutches staring back in horror at Fluffy's tow truck as he'd hobbled inside after his mother. And the expression on Mrs Ho's face, which said that she held me responsible for his distress. She knew I was to blame. And that we were now at war.

In my experience, there are two kinds of kids in this world.

The first bunch think money can buy everything. They're taught from the day they're born that they own the world and don't have to work for anything. When they meet people who don't speak and dress as they do, they think these people belong to an inferior tribe who should be kept where they belong, at their feet, where they can kick them. I met a lot of these kids at Trinity College. They didn't know how to think like me. I knew how to deal with them.

The other crowd knows that money can only buy some things. It can't buy you smarts and it can't buy you parents who'll live together and love you more than anything else in the whole wide world. These kids know that anything worth something has to be earned honestly, and that just because people don't have money it doesn't make them ugly and stupid. One of these kids at Trinity College was my friend Melly. I knew she was the best friend I could ever hope to have.

Then there was Sebastian, who was one of a kind. And when I was with Sebastian, I didn't know what to think at all.

Nine

I dress myself for war on Monday. My armour is a bit thin. Fluffy shakes his head and says he's really, really sorry, but unless he can track the tramp man down and reclaim our laundry, I'm going to have to wear civvies to school until he can buy me a new uniform.

He checks the tin stuffed with cash for a rainy day and shakes it mournfully. It's bucketing down but the tin is empty.

I shake my head and get the navy-blue school bag out of the broom cupboard where Fluffy had stuffed it during our big spring clean on Saturday. I shove it back inside and take my multicoloured satchel instead. If I'm going to die by the wrathful hand of Mrs Ho today, at least it's going to be in style.

The traffic lights at all the intersections in the eastern suburbs of Jozi are out of order and Fluffy gets me to school half an hour late. He then flies off to join the other vultures who are perched in prime positions to take full advantage of the road rage of late drivers, jammed back to back along the roads, bliksemming the dead traffic lights with multicoloured curses.

I meet Melly at the gate. She's huffing and puffing and in a terrible state about being late for school. Her position as class monitor makes it imperative for her to set a good example.

She smacks her head when she sees me in civvies. 'Oh no, I messed up. I forgot it was civvies day today.' She says I look really nice and admires my jeans and the oversized shirt I'm wearing (Fluffy's last clean one).

I tell Melly she didn't mess up at all. Fluffy made a mess over the weekend and donated my school uniforms to the poor people by mistake. I'm now without the regulation school threads.

Melly says poor old me. Then she says I must look on the bright side: I'll get all new stuff.

From my cash-strapped position, I can't see the bright side, or any new school clothes. But I do see Mrs Ho lurking in the corridor handing out detention notes to all latecomers.

She looks at Melly and shakes her head. 'This is so disappointing. You of all people!'

Melly goes red and wheezes on and on about the traffic lights. Mrs Ho ignores Melly's sobs and gives her a detention note anyway. She warns her to steer clear of bad influences. They can 'drag you down'.

Mrs Ho then looks down at me and drags me off to the Lost Property Box where she makes me change into someone else's manky uniform. She hands me a detention note and another note addressed to Fluffy. The woman won't give up.

The lessons before break drag. Sitting solo in front of the class, I miss the breathless company of Melly. I keep my head down in *New Moon* and try to ignore the conversations around me. Conversations that are all about me.

'She's wearing Tiffney's old dress.'

'She's got Damien's old sweater.'

And then they laugh like sick baboons about Britney's old socks and toe jam and athlete's foot. I'm not laughing.

Call me Antisocial. Call me Reclusive. Call me Stand-offish. But I am alienated by these creepy kids in my class. Dumb kids who need their parents to pay school fees to get them into Trinity College. Cretins who think Marco Polo's the cute guy they can never catch in the swimming pool.

I escape into the quad at break, feeling down in the dumps, hoping to find my friend Melly. I'm hiding out near the boys' toilets when I see him. And then he sees me.

He raises one eyebrow and crooks his finger. At me. He has smelt my blood. It's Edward the vampire.

He says to me, 'Bella.'

I say to him, 'Bas.'

I'm glad I'm the only person in the world whose mind Sebastian and Edward the vampire can't read, because the inside of my head is a jumble of words that have my right and left brains in a dangerous muddle.

Sebastian and his friends are playing a game and bouncing a cigarette. He offers me a drag but I decline (politely). I'm not big on group saliva. He asks me if I want to play. I definitely want to play. 'What are the rules?' I ask.

Sebastian says there are very few rules, which is how he likes his games. And I could get hurt. I might bleed. The blood rushes to my head and drowns out the cries of alarm from my left brain. I say I most definitely want to play.

Sebastian takes my hand. His hands are warm, not cold like Edward the vampire's. He holds out my hand in front of him and says, 'After the count of five, Bella, name in alphabetical order . . .' He pauses and thinks for a moment. 'Brands.'

My five seconds are up and I start: 'Audi, Bentley, Cadillac, Datsun . . .'

As I reel off the brand names of cars I know (because I'm in the fortunate situation of having a father in the automobile industry), Sebastian scratches the top of my hand over and over again in the same spot with his nail. It's long and sharpened to a point, like one of those guys who play guitar.

Two boys standing next to us are playing as well: names of blue-chip companies on the stock exchange. 'ABSA, BIDVest . . .' They're in the fortunate situation of having fathers who make a killing on the stock market and not on the roads.

The faster I can say the words, the less time Sebastian has to rip a bloody groove into the back of my hand. I finish with 'Zastava' and smile triumphantly. The back of my hand is bleeding. I have been marked by Edward the vampire. My left brain screams in pain and tells me I've lost my marbles.

Sebastian smiles at me. 'You're good.'

I smile back and say, 'You're bad.'

Sebastian lights another cigarette and passes it to me as I hear that familiar huffing and puffing at my back.

'You're smoking!' It's Melly. She looks at me the same way Mom looks at Fluffy when she's pretending to be a reformed smoker.

Sebastian is looking at Melly like she's fresh meat. He asks her if she wants to play a game.

Melly shakes her head. Oh no, she knows *that* game. It's stupid and dangerous. No one in their right mind would play such a sick game.

Melly looks at me for support. Then she looks at the back of my hand. Oh no.

Sebastian tells her she's chicken.

Melly says she is so not chicken. She looks at me again for my backing, but I look between Melly and Sebastian and then I tell Melly she's yellow.

Melly goes red and holds out her hand while Sebastian counts to five: girls' names.

Sebastian has gouged out a piece of flesh on the back of Melly's hand before she can get past April-May.

'April-May . . . April-May . . . April-May . . .' Melly squeaks pitifully at me.

I turn away. I won't help her. She needs to move on to Bella. The cigarette in my hand burns down and I steel myself by flicking cigarette ash all over my shoes.

Sebastian's sharp nail is doing his worst to the back of Melly's hand when I hear those footsteps coming at us down the corridor with military force. *Tap-tap-tap*. The boys scatter into the safety of the toilets and Melly and me are left to confront Mrs Ho.

Call her Loyal. Call her Faithful. Call her A Wet Dog. Call her whatever you want, but Melly doesn't blow the whistle on Sebastian and me. Instead, she holds her bleeding paw behind her back and takes her punishment like a trooper.

Mrs Ho rips the cigarette out of my hand and kills it

on the floor in a hostile onslaught. *Tap-tap-tap*. Then she gives us a blasting from hell about the dangers of smoking. And three hours' detention. And notes to our parents about us breaking the no-smoking rule. Finally she takes me aside and says, 'Caught bunking.' She jabs her finger against my chest and says, 'Caught smoking.' I want to tell her that I never was. Not even a puff. I was just holding it. But she wouldn't believe me and I've stopped caring. She walks away as she says, 'Three strikes and you're out of Trinity College.'

On our way back to class, I drop the note to Fluffy into the paper recycling bin along with the other two Mrs Ho gave me earlier that morning.

I see Sebastian standing outside in the quad. His bronze hair sparkles with diamonds as the rain drizzles down. He winks at me with those icy green eyes.

I try to ignore the tears that are drizzling down Melly's face. I pooh-pooh Melly when she tells me that Sebastian is a delinquent, a hooligan, a punk and a slacker. She won't hang out with Sebastian and his crowd. And I shouldn't either. I should stick with her. He's a rule-breaker, a 'dangerous influence'. He'll drag me down.

It is those last words which stop me from taking Melly's hand. They are the same ones Mrs Ho had used to describe me that morning. Coming from Melly they cut deeper than Sebastian's nail on my skin.

I gaze instead at the wound on my hand and push Melly away when she tries to put antiseptic on my injury.

It is no longer Melly and me. I belong with Sebastian now.

Cold Fact No. 8

Your left lung is smaller than your right lung, to make room for your heart.

Ten

I read my horoscope every morning in *The Times* and Fluffy reads the weather report. The newspaper is one of the assets Mom and Fluffy divided when they split – she got to keep the *Sunday Times* and we get the daily paper that comes free with the subscription.

My horoscope is a challenge to my ditzy right brain: *You need to make a judgment . . . you need to make a decision and stick to it so that you can move on with the rest of your life. Instinct is being biased by prejudice. Logic may help more than you expect today.*

Fluffy's weather report tells us that there's a twenty per cent chance of rain. But that's no reason for me to look so glum, he tells me. He's got a plan to access some cash and buy me a decent set of school uniforms. Fluffy says he's got a couple of tricks up his sleeve – and then he gives me a crafty look.

My scheme for the day is to shaft Mrs Ho. Her notes

91

to Fluffy have been cluttering up the school's paper recycling bin all week and I'm not sure how much longer I can hold her off. Her advance into my territory is relentless.

One of the advantages of coming from a rubbish school is that I've learnt all the tricks about dealing with troublesome teachers (and parents who won't realise that they love each other; and fat-gut boyfriends who come between them). But I know my horoscope is correct. I cannot win my war against Mrs Ho with childish tricks. I must deploy sophisticated logic and planning to triumph over her. I need Mrs Ho to pack her bags and leave Trinity College for good, before she strikes me down with a hat trick and gets me expelled.

I take an old bottle and fill it with bits of Mrs Ho's hair, which I'd carefully extracted from the back of her chair in class the day before. I add a couple of threads from her skirt and an old tissue she'd discarded in the classroom bin. I bury the bottle in the garden after chanting a few hexes. I start my day's battle fortified by my war charms.

I manage to make it through the last day of the week without getting taken down by Mrs Ho's fire. At the end of the day Melly asks if I want to hang out at her place for the weekend. I shrug her off and tell her I'm busy. I've got to get busy with my plan to influence Mrs Ho's fate.

I fast-track it to Willie's Wreckers to make use of the available weaponry there. My weapons consist of a typewriter, a bunch of careers sections from the newspapers and a fax machine. And Sharleen, who staffs the office and drinks a lot of strong coffee while she waits for the tow trucks to limp home with the wrecked cars.

Sharleen has worked for Willie's Wreckers for twenty-seven years. She says she's seen things with this pair of eyes that only God and his angels should ever see. If Fluffy stays in the job as long as she has, his eyes too will become dulled to the pain and misery of people who don't observe the keep right while overtaking rule.

Sharleen's eyes are the colour of the fish that Ishmael sometimes brings over to our house. They are cold and lifeless and battered.

I get busy with the newspapers and start hammering away at the typewriter. Sharleen says I'm wasting my time. There are just no jobs. No jobs in Fluffy's line of work. I must give up on sending off his curriculum vitae.

I want to court-martial Sharleen for undermining morale. I tell her I'm working on a project for my favourite teacher. I'm not here yet again to try and get Fluffy gainfully employed at a newspaper company. I'm here for Mrs Ho.

I spend the afternoon responding to job advertisements on behalf of Mrs Ho. She and me are applying for positions as Deputy Principal at a range of Jozi schools. Then I emigrate Mrs Ho to Cape Town and Bloemfontein. When vacancies at schools dry up, I apply for jobs as a game ranger, a chef and a matron at a mental hospital. I want Mrs Ho to be flexible. Times are tough in the job market.

I give Mrs Ho's cell number as a contact for her future employers. I'd extracted this from Sharleen after she'd told me that Mrs Ho had called seven times during the day – leaving her cell number for Fluffy to call her on.

I fax though Mrs Ho's applications while I drink Ricoffy with Sharleen and wait for Fluffy to scrape the roadkill off the Soweto Highway and come back to the office.

He comes back flushed with success. He shakes his head when I ask him. No, no pile-ups, no drunks, no under-age drivers wreaking mayhem with the taxis on the highway. He's got two large parcels from the uniform stockists.

Call me Suspicious. Call me Distrustful and Wary. But the last time I checked Fluffy's rainy-day tin it shook like a Polo in a collision with a Bedford truck. Sharleen also casts her fishy eyes over Fluffy's purchases.

Fluffy shakes his head. He didn't steal them, he didn't

rob a bank, he didn't hock Willie's tow truck. No. He bought my new uniforms on credit.

Credit! Debt! I nearly take the two bags of clothes and beat Fluffy to a pulp. Does he not read his horoscope? Didn't he see today that: *Frugality is the mother of all virtues. Don't spend what you don't have. Instant gratification is the father of all ills. Avoid the debt trap.*

Fluffy says it's cool. He's got a new credit card courtesy of his medical aid. He only needs to pay it off next month.

Some people collect stamps. Others collect teachers' notes to their fathers. My father Fluffy collects credit cards. And at the end of the month he rolls over his debt like a Volksie beetle with a burst front tyre on the N12 to Kimberley.

Sharleen sighs and holds out her hand. Fluffy shakes his head and puts his hands behind his back until Sharleen skewers him with her fried-hake eyes. Then she takes his new credit card and feeds it into the shredder. 'The clothes are going back to the shop tomorrow,' she says. 'No argument.'

I'm trying to stop Fluffy from feeding Sharleen's lotto tickets into the shredder when Ishmael arrives. He is heavily laden with fish and chips and a crate of Fanta to wash down his good fortune.

He has some sensational news. And he tells us in between spitting bits of fish bone out into Sharleen's paper clip holder.

As Ishmael talks I find myself choking. And then, declining all offers of Fanta to help me stop gagging, I run through to the bathroom to park my lunch.

There are ways of winning a war. There is the American way, where you napalm defenceless villages and burn all the crops so that the civilians starve to death (or resort to eating grass to stay alive). And then there's the April-May February way, which says that there are rules in war. You must take on opponents of equal strength and stature and use your brain and cunning to defeat them. You don't stick pins into old Barbie dolls and resort to trying to kill off your teacher with hexes and spells.

By the time I'm finished in the bathroom, Ishmael is telling his story for the second time.

'The Fanta truck just took out that teacher's car.' Ishmael waves his hand across Sharleen's desk and brings it down with a thud. 'Smack-bang into the barrier on the R24 to Edenvale. There was Fanta all over the tarmac. It was running orange with blood.' He points to the crate of Fanta on the floor – his salvaged booty. 'That teacher of yours won't be around for a while,' he says to me. 'And that car . . .' Ishmael jerks his greasy thumb towards the Toyota Corolla that is clinging listlessly to the back of his tow truck.

I don't hear the rest of Ishmael's story. I'm back in the bathroom with my head over the toilet bowl.

I wanted Mrs Ho out of my life. I wanted her to leave Trinity College. But God and your angels, shut your eyes on my vengeful plans, I never wanted Mrs Ho to be dead.

Cold Fact No. 9

You can overdose on coffee. It takes ten grams of caffeine in one sitting to kill a person, which translates as between eighty and a hundred cups of coffee. This is pretty hard to do.

Eleven

I spend the next day hanging out with Sebastian and his pack in the park across the road from school. I don't know what the day has in store for me because the daily newspaper doesn't come on Saturdays – my future is a blank slate.

Meanwhile, my soul feels like a grey, barren piece of granite. It feels like I'm going to hell with Edward the vampire and his psychic sister Alice and the whole bunch of them in *New Moon* for killing off Mrs Ho with my bloodthirsty spells. It's a balmy Jozi day, but my body feels freezing cold.

Sebastian says I need to take a chill pill. I look way too uptight for the weekend. He and his pals have lit a bonfire. They found three rubbish bags full of rags abandoned by some bergie under the trampoline and the fire is just awesome.

'Cool,' I say as I watch my old school uniforms and

Fluffy's favourite dressing gown go up in flames. I feel like throwing myself into the fire along with them. As, it seems, does the sad tramp man when he comes back to see his loot gone to hell in the inferno.

Sebastian and his friends spend a lot of time playing on their cellphones and listening to music on their iPods. They order pizza from Mr Delivery and then get fully into the park apparatus and do some swinging. They go as high as they can, and when they come short and fall hard on the concrete they howl like wolves and say, 'Awesome!'

They keep the bonfire going with the pizza boxes and play a game called chicken where they compete to see who can hold his hand over the flames for the longest. I win a couple of times against Sebastian. I think I need to get used to the burning fires of hell.

Sebastian says, 'You're hot.'

I tell him I'm cold. But my hands are red and blistered. They look like I've got a severe case of Melly's pink-hand syndrome.

After a few hours of hanging and falling off the swing and burning my hands and feeling dangerous and brave enough to face the world again I decide to go home.

I leave Sebastian and his crew playing chicken on the see-saw – whoever jumps off first will make the winner's coccyx crack when he hits the ground – and take an overpacked taxi home (to see how fate has decided to treat me). We narrowly miss getting hit in a freak accident by a two-seater Piper Cherokee, which ploughs head-on into a bakkie on the way to Krugersdorp airport (miraculously, no fatalities).

I get home safe only to find a Toyota Corolla parked in the driveway next to Fluffy's tow truck. The car doesn't look like it's been in a collision with a Fanta truck. In fact, there's not a scratch on the bodywork. I conclude that I must have died and Mrs Ho has driven to our pearly gates to consult with Saint Peter as to whether I should be sent down to the rubbish school called hell while she stays and hangs out with the trinity in a college called heaven.

But Mrs Ho isn't bending Saint Peter's ear. No. Mrs Ho is sitting in my kitchen bending Fluffy's ears, which are as red as my hands. And there's not a scratch on her body either.

I pinch the back of my hand and nearly hit the roof in agony when I realise that Mrs Ho is not dead. And Fluffy's puffing away on a Texan Plain, so I know all is not well.

I greet Mrs Ho with a nod and surreptitiously touch the back of her arm. She's not a ghost. She's flesh and blood, and a bit bony.

'What a terrible thing to have happened.' Fluffy looks up at me. 'Did you know about this, April?'

'What?' I ask Fluffy.

Fluffy tells me that Mrs Ho has been telling him about the accident yesterday, where one of the teachers from Trinity College was involved in a collision with a Fanta truck.

I tell Fluffy that I was there when Ishmael told us all about it.

'Poor old Finger,' Fluffy says and shakes his head.

'Finger?'

Apparently Mr Goosen had been driving along on the highway, clutching a cigarette in his four-fingered hand, when he'd decided to overtake a slow taxi. For some reason, that day, he'd forgotten that he didn't have an index finger, so although he thought he had, he hadn't indicated. And that's when he'd been taken out by the Fanta truck.

Mrs Ho reassures Fluffy that Mr Goosen is fine. Only two fingers broken on his left hand and three-quarters of the zap finger on his right hand chopped off for good.

Fluffy shakes his head and rambles on about what a brave man Finger was to save the newborn twins from Neville the vicious dog, only to lose another finger in yet another tragic incident.

Mrs Ho looks like she thinks Fluffy's terminally mad and tells us that, confronted by mortality, old Finger has decided not to wait until he turns a century and is taking retirement from the school with immediate effect. As soon as he's out of hospital he'll be off to Clarens and his B & B in his new car.

My face is a picture, Fluffy tells me.

I'm picturing never again having Finger zap me with his middle finger in class during roll-call. I'm envisaging being able to read Stephenie Meyer in his classes unsupervised for the rest of the term.

Mrs Ho says that there's no reason for me to look so concerned, she'll be standing in for Finger and teaching History until his replacement can be found.

I think Ishmael is so history for misleading me. For his misinformation, his hogwash, his downright Goebbels-like treachery in allowing me to let my guard down and believe that I was safe from Mrs Ho he should be battered and deep-fried in a vat full of fish oil.

Mrs Ho looks at her watch and says she can't stay long. The reason she popped in after Fluffy never returned any of her calls was to discuss April-May's future at Trinity College.

Fluffy rubs his red ears and says I need to make myself scarce. I can go and hang with Mrs Ho's son who's in the back, playing in the garden.

I leave the two of them with their heads together, conspiring on how to hang me out to dry for bunking, for smoking, for reading *Twilight* in class, for not wearing the regulation school uniform . . . Mrs Ho's list of my transgressions is criminal.

Mrs Ho's son's name is Sam. That's it. No Sam-Sung

or Sam-Mule or anything ridiculous to indicate that Mr and Mrs Ho had been arguing from the day he was born. Just Sam Ho. Seven years old.

His face lights up when he sees me and he asks if I'll play with him.

I don't feel like playing nice with Just Sam Ho. I think about teaching him how to smoke. I contemplate playing the scratch-scratch hand game. I consider daring him to jump from the top branch of the sour-sour tree. I suggest hopscotch.

Sam Ho points to his crutches and makes a face.

'Life's not fair,' I tell him. 'Get used to it.'

He says he'll have an unfair advantage.

'Let's play,' I say.

I chalk out the blocks and throw a button into the first square. I'm the polite hostess – I say he can go first. I watch Sam Ho swing and hop and glide all the way to the last square and then bounce and sway and slide all the way back again. He says it's my turn.

After Sam Ho has thrashed me hollow, I suggest we play the rope game.

Sam Ho points to his crutches and asks if I'm sure. He has an unfair handicap.

'Life's not a bowl of cherries,' I tell him. 'Suck it up.'

I tie the one end of the rope to the sour-sour tree and let him go first. At first I go slow and Sam Ho double-jumps at each swing of the rope. Then I swing the rope as fast as I can and Sam Ho hops and bops at the speed of light until my arms are aching. Then it's my turn.

Sam Ho turns the rope slowly and lets me have three new starts when I fall down at the count of six, at the count of two and then I'm eating rotten berries off the ground before he even gets to swing the rope. He offers me his crutches. 'I think your mom's calling you,' I say.

Fluffy and me see our guests out at the front gate. Then Fluffy sits me down at the kitchen table and after he's finished with me I feel like I've been through another bout of bouncing and skipping and falling down and getting thrashed by a seven-year-old boy called Just Sam Ho.

'Smoking!' Fluffy says, lighting a Texan Plain with the burning stompie of another. His hands are shaking and I can see he's a bit mad at me. 'Caught smoking!' he continues, dragging hard on the Texan Plain. 'You're on your last warning, April. And Mrs Ho says that she doesn't want to see you at school again without the *right* uniform.' He points his finger at me.

I point my finger back. 'No problem,' I say. 'There's the new stuff you bought me.' I'm good to go.

Fluffy frowns and says Sharleen took the new uniforms back to the shop. But – and Fluffy smiles happily – he managed to track the tramp man down yesterday. He bribed him with his favourite dressing gown and some shirts to get him to bring my school uniforms back. Fluffy looks at the clock on the kitchen wall. 'He should be here any minute now,' he says.

My blistered hands start to itch as I see Fluffy's dressing gown and my bursary at Trinity College going up in flames.

Cold Fact No. 10

If there are two or more ways to do something, and one of those ways can result in a catastrophe, someone will do it. (Murphy's Law)

Twelve

Jonathan Cainer in *The Times* horoscope warns me on Monday to be careful: *Your magical powers are at a premium today. Be careful what you wish for. You may just get it.*

In the back garden I carefully dig up the bottle containing Mrs Ho's hair. I add a tube of lipstick she left behind over the weekend, a thread from the laces of Sam Ho's takkies and his half-eaten Marie biscuit. Then I pack the jar full of flowers, say some good luck incantations over the bottle and hang it by a piece of string in the sour-sour tree.

I am full of goodwill towards Mrs Ho. I'm wishing her the best of luck in succeeding with her application for Deputy Principal to the school in Cape Town, where it rains in winter and is packed with German tourists who drive on the right (wrong) side of the road in summer.

I also wish prosperity on a downcast Fluffy, who says that my Lost Property school uniform looks like a car wreck and that if he ever gets his hands on that no-good tramp man he'll make him wish he was jobless and home-less and without two cents to rub together.

Melly is panting outside the school gates when I arrive. I try and slip past her but she grabs me with those bright pink hands and gives me a parcel of clothes. 'Here. These are my school uniforms from last year,' she says.

Call me Proud. Call me Arrogant. Call me Uppity or Snooty or whatever it is you want to call me, but I draw the line at certain things. I tell Melly huffily that I'm good, thank you very much, and she can give her old clothes to the poor people who need them because I certainly don't. Jonathan Cainer and me are convinced that the gods are smiling on Mrs Ho. She'll be off to Cape Town before Melly can say charity for the bursary kid and I'll be able to dress as I please for the rest of my life. I wish Melly a good day and tell her to buzz off.

Melly shoves the clothes into my arms and runs as fast as her tiny little lungs can propel her into the school building. I stuff the clothes down to the bottom of my navy-blue Lost Property satchel and hang out with Sebastian until the bell rings for class.

We play the scratch-scratch game and I name the signs of the zodiac in alphabetical order before he has time to break the swollen cluster of blisters on the back of my burnt hand. 'You're a lucky witch, Bella,' Sebastian says.

'If you only knew, Bas,' I tell him. 'If only you knew.'

I spend the whole day cashing in on my lucky horoscope by making spells for all my loved ones.

My wish for Mom and Sarel is that they get trapped in a lift and decide after three days that their cohabitory relationship must come to an end.

I wish that Fluffy meets a nice girl who's reached her goal weight and knows how to scrub dirty pots and do the laundry. And that Fluffy doesn't want to cohabit with her and calls her his best friend (after Ishmael).

I wish a hundred times that Mrs Ho gets the position of Deputy Principal – in Jozi, Cape Town or Bloemfontein (I'm not fussy).

I wish that Melly would stop looking at me with those wishful eyes. I'm busy!

At break I zigzag around the netball court, tracing the magical signs of my coven as I wish that Fluffy's drivers on the N17 to Springs hit it unlucky today, so that I can get a cellphone and an iPod and become part of Sebastian's cool set.

Then, before the break bell rings, I wish that a raven would swoop down and rip the tongues out of Britney and Tiffney and Damien's mouths and fly off to join Finger in Clarens. They have cornered me on the netball court and are doing what they know best: beating up on the bursary kid.

'That's Damien's sweater. You stole it, April-May.'

'Those are Britney's socks. I'm telling on you, April-May.'

'That's Tiffney's school dress. Strip, April-May.'

They call me names. Like Brains, Swot, Inte-Lektshual, Einstein – all the ugly words they know for kids like me who are smarter than them. And faster too . . . because I make it safely to the girls' toilets before the grey goopy matter between their ears can figure out I'm gone.

I strip off the Lost Property clothes and change into Melly's old rags, ripping the price tags off the clothes in the process. Dof old Melly! I imagine her walking around school the previous year with the prices on her clothes hanging out for everyone to see. That is before I figure out that the clothes have a 'new' kind of smell to them. And I wish with all my disloyal heart that Melly will recover from her sleep apnoea and learn to breathe through her nose like regular kids. And that her pink hands will get enough oxygen to change to a normal pink person's colour.

I dump the stupid kids' clothes back in the Lost Property Box and make it to class just as Mrs Ho is making a BIG announcement. I don't mind that I've missed half of it – Jonathan Cainer and me already know all about it.

I wait for the class to start their slow clap to congrat-ulate Mrs Ho on her new job as Deputy Principal in Cape Town. I wish her a safe journey on the N1 to the Mother

City with Just Sam Ho and her lovely memories of Trinity College and me. I think good thoughts about Mrs Ho.

Mrs Ho carries on babbling. She says that it's an opportunity for all aspirant writers to shine. She looks at me and nods approvingly at my smart new uniform. 'Nice to see you've turned over a new leaf, April-May.'

I want to tell her how nice it is for her that she's shoving off to Cape Town, but the stars wink at me and say, *All in good time*.

I try and keep my impatience at bay for the rest of the day and keep faith with Jonathan Cainer. He's a certified astrologer. He's an authority on the stars. He's no snake-oil salesman, peddling lies. He's not like Mom.

Mom who is sitting with Sarel and Fluffy when I get home from school.

Fluffy looks at me warily and says Mom and Sarel have some BIG news to tell me. I look at the happy couple and see that they appear safe and unfazed by their three-day ordeal, trapped in the lift. I nod sorrowfully at Mom. 'I know,' I say. 'I predicted it.'

Mom tells me that I could not have predicted *this* – and she holds out her left hand and points to the ring.

Sarel says that the real engagement ring is locked away in the safe back home in Pretoria. He wants Mom to wear a very modest cluster of diamonds so as not to tempt hijackers and thieves.

115

Mom says Sarel proposed to her in the lift between floors at Woolworths three days ago. 'It took me quite by surprise,' she says. 'Aren't you surprised, May?'

I say it's magical.

The happy twosome finally leave Fluffy and me slumped over the kitchen table smoking Texan Plains and eating spoonfuls of jam. I'm feasting on Koo, getting bug-eyed from all the sugar. Fluffy's feeding his addiction to carcinogens – courtesy of British American Tobacco.

Fluffy says it's been the worst day of his life. 'It seemed to me all day that there were forces at work out to get me.' He holds his head in his hands and says he made a real killing today. There'll be enough money for iPods and cellphones and school uniforms and fish and chips for the rest of the month.

I thank my lucky stars and Jonathan Cainer.

Fluffy doesn't look very happy about it, though. His eyes have the same glassy stare as Sharleen's. He says he saw today what only God and his angels should ever see. He doesn't know how much longer he can continue in this terrible, terrible job. 'I thought I could become hardcore like Ishmael and the other wreckers. But every day it feels like I'm losing bits of my soul.'

He goes to bed without eating any noodles and I hear him pacing all night, chain-smoking his Texan Plains and finishing off the jam.

I want to tell Fluffy that he needs to trust in the stars. Mrs Ho is going to get a new job and he's going to get a new best friend who will clean the pots and do our laundry. But I can't sleep either. I'm going over all the things I wished for. Two of them came true: Mom and Sarel are stopping cohabiting to go legal, which is sort of my fault (maybe I wasn't as clear with the stars as I should have been), and I'm getting a cellphone.

I don't know why Fluffy and me are feeling so miserable.

Cold Fact No. 11

In 2002, British comedian Dave Gorman spent forty days and nights living entirely by his horoscope, to prove once and for all if there was any truth in it. Jonathan Cainer made him stand on one leg in Covent Garden with his foot in a bucket of water, a satsuma in one hand and some breakfast cereal in the other, singing 'God Save the Queen' backwards and balancing three books on his head.

Thirteen

I wake up feeling tired and gritty from lack of sleep.

My street is not the quietest in Africa. At three o'clock every morning the two dogs from next door run up and down the road chasing their friend dog who comes to visit from another block. They do this for about two hours while people from the other houses throw bottles at them and tell them to bladdie voetsak.

Then at five o' clock in the morning, the man across the road moves his kombi away from the entrance to his garage so that he can drive his work car out. Then he moves the kombi into the garage. The kombi has a faulty exhaust, which he says he won't fix unless we pay. Apparently that will teach us for wanting to lie around and sleep all day.

Half an hour later, the two dogs next door go for yet another training session for The Comrades and chase *The Times* delivery man down the street, trying to rip a rubber breakfast from his bicycle tyres.

And then it's Fluffy hammering on my bedroom door, saying it's time to get up and don't make me miss rush hour today.

Fluffy looks as poorly as I feel. He says he hardly slept a wink all night, thinking about those crazy drive-on-the-right-hand-side German tourists and the busload of kids on a rugby tour . . . and then he rubs his hand across his eyes and says he shouldn't be telling me these things, it will damage my soul.

I tell Fluffy that things will get better. He has Ishmael and me, and a new best friend waiting for him around the corner. Fluffy's face says that he doesn't have Mom any more. Sarel has her. And, he says, he really, really needs to move on now. And with that he leaves me outside the school gates.

Melly is waiting for me as usual. And so is Sam Ho, who says he wants to hang out with me again. He thinks I'm his new best friend. I tell him to hop off and leave me alone.

I leave him with Melly. They can be new best friends.

My day doesn't improve. First it's double Biology (Mrs Ho). She makes us dissect a frog. We have to get into pairs and choose a frog from the fridge in the lab. Melly waves a pink hand at me, but I do the maths and figure that there are twenty-one kids in the class, which means that one of us has to go it alone. That's me.

Melly gets stuck with Damien, who spends the double period slipping his ruler under her bum, so she cries and gets into trouble. Meanwhile I get stuck with Mrs Ho, who says she'll make up the numbers.

I get a sense of Mrs Ho's mettle by the way she makes me use the scalpel to mutilate the frog's chest so that I can count the chambers of its heart (there are three); and the way she makes me dissect its eyelids to count the membranes (there are three); and the way she forces me to carve up its left leg to expose and measure its elongated ankle bone (it's three centimetres long).

After this I tell Mrs Ho that I'll hold the frog down; it's her turn to play butcher. I make her chop up the frog's nether regions to look for its tail (non-existent, only tadpoles have tails). If frogs had blood, the lab counter would've been swimming in the stuff by the time Mrs Ho and me are done.

After Biology it's double History (Mrs Ho). Mrs Ho tells us to get into pairs and role play being Paul Kruger and his arch-enemy Cecil John Rhodes in their war to gain control of the Boer Republic. We stay in our pairs from the Biology class – Damien has Melly cornered under her desk – and so I get to play Paul Kruger with Mrs Ho.

Mrs Ho keeps wanting to talk about the discovery of gold and the Jameson Raid, but I'm way ahead of her. So far ahead, in fact, that I'm exiled in Clarens, living at Finger's B & B and teaching him how to shoot a gun with three fingers and make biltong.

Mrs Ho says I (Paul Kruger) was exiled to Clarens in Switzerland (where I died in 1904), not Clarens in the Free State. We spend the lesson arguing about geography. She's making me sick. Next thing she's going to try and tell me that the big guy in the sky was born in Bethlehem in the Free State. This woman is going to be the death of me.

After break it's double English (Mrs Ho). The only consolation is that by the time English arrives I think Mrs Ho is sicker of me than I am of her. She makes the class settle down and get on with the essays for the creative writing competition.

This was the BIG announcement I half missed yesterday. The winner of the competition gets to meet Stephenie Meyer and will spend a week in Forks, Washington with Edward the vampire.

The topic of the essay is 'My Best Friend'. I know I'm going to win this competition and get to drive around in Bella's truck in the rain and hang out with Alice the clairvoyant and the cool gang.

I'm two hundred words into my essay about my best friend Sebastian when I hear Melly panting at my shoulder. She says she wants to measure my height and check out the exact shade of brown of my eyes so that she can describe me accurately in her essay.

'I'm busy,' I tell her.

'Please,' she says.

I tell her to please, please leave me in peace, I'm trying to concentrate.

I'm writing about how Sebastian is the best friend a person could ever have. He plays the scratch-scratch game with me and taught me how to smoke a Camel, which I'm not very good at because it makes my teeth feel funny. I need to try harder.

I write about how Sebastian lets me tag along to the park with him and his pack and doesn't tease me too much about not having a cellphone and an iPod. And I'm just describing the thing that Sebastian does with his bare foot, when he puts his cigarette out, when the bell rings. I quickly finish off my essay with a description of Sebastian's blunt, gapped teeth, which I make clear to Stephenie Meyer do not mean that he's *not* a vampire.

Mrs Ho says we can finish off our essays next week and then she'll submit them to the competition en masse. I'm done. She can send mine off whenever she likes. (If she's still around and not on her way to her new school in Cape Town.)

After school I watch Sebastian and his mates play ambush in the quad with the fire extinguishers. I get caught in the crossfire once or twice but I don't mind too much.

I spot Melly and Sam Ho hiding in the parking lot with some other kids who don't want to play ambush. The gang cheers Sebastian on when he manages to corner Melly outside the tuck shop, though Sam Ho manages to hop away before he too gets covered in foam.

By the time I get home I'm hyper from all the fun. Fluffy's in better spirits too. And so is Mrs Ho.

The pair of them are sitting around the kitchen table and Fluffy says, 'Look who I bumped into around the corner.' He mashes his hair and doesn't catch my eye, which is asking him what the heck is *she* doing here?

Mrs Ho asks July (alias Fluffy) if she can have another cup of rooibos, and Fluffy leaps up and puts the kettle on for Julia (aka Mrs Ho). Fluffy's eyes are bright and no longer fishy and battered like Sharleen's.

I nod suspiciously at Mrs Ho and go and check out the state of our dirty pots. They are scrubbed, dried and put away in the cupboard. My heart leaps into the back of my throat. Either Fluffy's been busy or another pair of hands has been in our kitchen sink. I go and check on the laundry basket in the bathroom and breathe out with relief. It's still full of Fluffy's odd socks. Either Fluffy's been tardy as usual, or meddlesome hands haven't quite made it into the laundry basket. Either way, I've got time to put a stop to this nonsense.

Fluffy says Mrs Ho and him are drinking to Mrs Ho's success. She's just received some wonderful news. She's been appointed to the post of Deputy Principal.

I hug Fluffy and then I hug Mrs Ho and give her a quick nip on her neck in my excitement. If Jonathan Cainer had been around I would have hugged him too. My wishes have been answered: Mrs Ho and Sam Ho are moving on to Cape Town.

'I know Mr Goosen will be pleased for me. And I feel honoured to have been chosen to fill his position at Trinity College,' Mrs Ho says.

I say I have things I have to do and I leave the kitchen. I go and rip up my Jonathan Cainer scrapbook – where I had been collecting his words of wisdom – and then I smash the bottle containing the bits of Mrs Ho's and Sam Ho's lives, swinging happily in the sour-sour tree.

I take one of Fluffy's Texan Plains from the emergency stash and weigh up the odds of smoking it to the end without throwing up. My luck's been rubbish of late so I go for broke and snap it in half instead.

Fluffy sees Mrs Ho to her car and then comes and finds me. He hands me a package and says I'm now officially connected. My new cellphone will mean that I can call Mom and my friends any time without having to run across the road to Mrs Barnard. Fluffy also has a new cellphone. He says I can call him any time too.

His phone rings and Fluffy answers. His eyes sparkle when he hears the voice on the other end. He tells the caller that he's looking forward to 'tomorrow night'.

When Fluffy ends the call he tells me he's taking a friend to the movies tomorrow night.

'What movie are you taking Ishmael and me to see?' I ask Fluffy.

But he says that he's taking his friend Julia to the movies tomorrow night and that I'm staying at home. It's just Fluffy and Mrs Ho. Not me.

Cold Fact No. 12

When a frog vomits it throws up its stomach first, so that it's dangling out of its mouth. The frog then uses its forearms to dig out all of the stomach's contents before swallowing the stomach back down again.

Fourteen

My word for today is 'spoilsport'. Call me Mean and Ugly and a Sore Loser or whatever the heck you please, but that's who I've decided to be today.

I'm resilient. I can put up with a lot of things. I can cope with Mrs Ho being made Deputy Principal at Trinity College. I can bear getting skopped back to my rubbish school in Pretoria. I can even tolerate Mom marrying Sarel the Bloodsucker. But there's one thing I will not deal with: Fluffy and Mrs Ho becoming new best friends (and having her clean my pots and wash Fluffy's socks).

Fluffy starts off bushy-tailed about his movie date with Mrs Ho – he spends an hour cleaning his tow truck until he can count his teeth in the body work – but then he gets all edgy and spends three hours in the bath, changes his shirt six times and cuts himself shaving (and uses my deodorant on his neck).

As Fluffy makes himself beautiful, I get busy. I set the

clock on the kitchen wall one hour fast and yell to Fluffy that if he doesn't hurry up Mrs Ho will be here before he's ready.

Fluffy comes out of the bathroom, looks at the clock and tells me that he's still got five minutes until she arrives to pick him up. He goes and brushes his teeth again, then he comes and sits at the kitchen table and breaks the rest of the Texan Plains in half. He tells me that Julia doesn't like smokers.

'Like Mom?' I ask him.

'Not a bit like your mother,' Fluffy replies, but then he goes very quiet.

Fluffy stares at the clock on the kitchen wall and his forehead goes crinkly. He glances outside – it's not raining, visibility on the roads should be perfect. No accidents today.

Fifteen minutes pass and Fluffy chews his nails all the way down. He says he's going to phone Julia to check if she's OK. She may have forgotten where we live.

Fluffy looks for his new cellphone but he can't find it because it's in the chilli jar where some sourpuss has stashed it. He asks me if he can borrow my new phone, please. I shake my head and say, sadly, 'No airtime.'

Then Fluffy's phone rings and he goes crazy trying to trace the ringtone to its hiding place. He finally finds it and shakes his head sadly at me.

It's Ishmael, phoning to wish Fluffy good luck on his date.

'No, she's not fat, she's perfect,' Fluffy tells Ishmael and says he has to make an urgent call so get off the line.

He phones Mrs Ho but she doesn't answer. She's probably in the bathroom, making herself beautiful for Fluffy. He leaves a message, giving her our address and detailed directions to the house. He tells her he can't wait.

Fluffy goes and gets his wallet and while he's gone I set his phone to mute. We don't need any more interruptions. And then I delete Mrs Ho's phone number from his contact list for good measure.

While the big hand on the clock ticks on, Fluffy paces up and down the kitchen. By Fluffy's time, she's half an hour late. By my calculations, she should be arriving in half an hour's time.

I take pity on Fluffy and tell him that she's obviously not going to make it. I'll go with him to movies instead. Somehow I have to get him out of the house before Mrs Ho arrives.

Fluffy says he thinks he'll call it a day and have an early night, but even as he says this the front doorbell rings and there's Mrs Ho. It seems she couldn't wait either.

While Fluffy answers the door, I remove his cash and movie clubcard from his wallet. As I do this I hear Mrs Ho telling Fluffy that she's sorry to be so early, but the babysitter couldn't come and she's stuck with Sam Ho. She says that she tried to call him earlier but he didn't pick up. Perhaps they can go to a movie another time? Sam Ho is at her side and he waves a crutch at me.

Fluffy looks at the kitchen clock, he looks at Mrs Ho's watch, then he looks at me and gives a disappointed shake of the head. He knows a very responsible young lady who would be only too happy to sit with Sam Ho while they go to the movies, he says.

'Who?' Mrs Ho asks, then she frowns at me and tells me not to take any chances with Sam Ho.

I tell her that we'll stay indoors and won't be playing hopscotch or the rope game or any other game where he's at a disadvantage. I'll play fair.

Then I suggest to Mrs Ho that she might like to freshen up before they leave and I point to the bathroom.

Fluffy catches my look. 'Not that hoary old chestnut,' he growls, and tells Mrs Ho that they should go immediately before she gets trapped by circumstances. They leave Sam Ho with the Grinch and take off.

Sam Ho immediately wants to know what I want to play.

'I don't want to play anything,' I tell him.

He calls me a party pooper, and I say that's exactly who I've decided to be today. I'm a Killjoy and a Wet Blanket as well.

I tell Sam Ho that he can make himself useful by cleaning the house and I go to my room and read *New Moon*.

Half an hour later Ishmael arrives. He says he told Fluffy that he would come and check on us. He's brought Chinese.

'Chinese? Where's the fish and chips?'

Ishmael says he thinks we all need a change. Just like Fluffy, we're moving on.

Sam Ho has a heart attack when he sees Ishmael. It seems they've met before. Ishmael tells me that eight months earlier he had the pleasure of meeting Mrs Ho and Sam Ho on the N3 to Durban. He shakes Sam Ho's hand and says he's so sorry about that beautiful Audi. It was a wreck. And for Sam Ho injuring his back and having to use crutches. He's also so sorry about Sam Ho's father. Sam Ho says he's so sorry too.

Ishmael leaves and we eat Chinese. Sam Ho has a bad reaction to the monosodium glutamate and has another heart attack, but I revive him by pouring a bucket of cold water over his head. I think my babysitting career and my bursary are going to hell.

Sam Ho goes and lies down and I pace. I look at the clock on the wall and I calculate that the movie should have been over two hours ago. Then I set the clock right and figure Fluffy's an hour late. What could they be doing?

They creep back into the house at midnight. I'm wide awake and waiting. 'Where the heck have you been?' I scream at Fluffy.

'And what the heck are *you* still doing up?' Fluffy retaliates. 'And hand over my cash and my movie clubcard!'

Fluffy packs Sam Ho and Mrs Ho into their car and I see them shake hands. And then Fluffy leans forward and kisses her on both cheeks, like an Italian person in a lame play written by a toothless old man.

When Fluffy comes back inside I'm waiting at the kitchen table, drumming my fingers.

'April, you're behaving like a brat,' he says.

I tell him I'm a sore loser.

He says that there are no winners and losers and that he's not playing games. And that I must stop this nonsense before I get hurt. He then tells me that he loves me more than anything else in the whole wide world. 'But I have to move on, April,' he says and tries to hug me.

I push him away. 'Are you going to marry Mrs Ho?' I ask him.

Fluffy shakes his head and says that he doesn't like to move that fast, but she's the best thing to have happened to him since he met Mom.

'What about Mom?' I ask Fluffy.

Fluffy says Mom has Sarel.

'And you have me,' I tell Fluffy. 'Or have you forgotten?'

Fluffy says that Mrs Ho and him are just friends.

I tell him that I know the signs. He kissed her cheek. Twice.

Fluffy throws up his hands. 'I'm going to bed,' he says. 'And if you don't like me moving on and having new friends you can move back to Pretoria and live with Mom and Sarel.' Then he goes to his bedroom and slams the door.

'I'll do just that,' I shout back. 'Just watch me.'

Cold Fact No. 13

A woman in China lost her hearing from kissing her boyfriend when a passionate kiss reduced pressure in her mouth, pulling out her eardrums and rupturing them.

Fifteen

I'm smart. Part of the reason for my sass is because I've benefited from my gene pool – a very smart father, and a mother who used to be clever before she decided to get hitched to Sarel the Leech.

The other part of my smarts comes from my environment – the pitiful fact that I don't have a computer, a television or any of the other toys that come with parents who have lots of cash and haven't split their assets. Because of my deprivation, I read a lot.

I know from reading everything I can lay my hands on that there are a lot of things that can cause accidents. For instance, one of the biggest causes of fatalities on the roads is speed. There are people in this world who kill off their loved ones and the families of people who they've never even met by driving too fast. Fluffy says these people are just plain brain-dead (before and after). Anyone with a bit of sense should know that the faster you smash into the back of an oil tanker when you're driving a Tazz, the more damage you're going to do. Force exerted on mass combined with increased velocity equals an accident. It's basic science.

Then there are people who like to do crazy things in their cars while driving. Fluffy has a story about this one woman travelling from Jozi to Pretoria in peak hour. She was texting her mother in Port Alfred, smoking a cigarette, picking her nose and trying to adjust the volume on her radio at the same time. She never saw the Datsun driver who was touching up her lipstick in the mirror while chatting on the cellphone at the William Nichol turnoff. She didn't get to see Fluffy when he arrived on the scene either.

Fluffy says these people who DWT (Drive While Texting) and DWD (Drive While Drunk) are just plain dumb. They cause accidents that should never happen. Things that could always have been prevented with a bit of sense and foresight.

Knowing what is dumb and not acting dumb are two different things. And as a smart kid, I should know the difference. But I leave my smarts in Fluffy's tow truck on the way to school today.

Sebastian is chilling in the quad when I get to school. His eyes are dark with excitement. He says he's got an awesome game planned for after school. It's dangerous. I may get hurt. I could get expelled.

I think of leaving Fluffy and Mrs Ho in Jozi and going back to Mom and Sarel in Pretoria and I tell Sebastian that I'm in the game of getting expelled.

'You're crazy, Bella,' Sebastian says.

I think I'm crazy about him.

After school I meet Sebastian and his crew in the quad outside the clock tower. They've taken off their school ties and are debating who will go first. They don't consult me. I'm just Bella, the bursary kid who hangs around Sebastian.

The only one who doesn't look scared stupid is Sebastian. They all hang back until I say I'll go first. Then they crowd around me and slap my hands and tell me that I'm crazy. I'm part of the tribe. And they laugh.

Getting to the top of the three-storey school building is puddysticks for me. I shimmy up the drainpipe on to the ledge of the first floor and then up the drainpipe to the next floor. I teeter on the ledge and look in at Mrs Ho's classroom window – they still haven't replaced the burglar bars the firemen ripped out when they were trying to spring her loose two weeks ago. I see Just Sam Ho sitting at his mother's desk, playing snap with Melly. I don't wave.

I claw my way up the next drainpipe to the next ledge and then pull myself on to the roof. I'm the king of the castle!

I watch the kids messing around in the quad below and try to get up some courage for the next leg.

Getting to the top of the clock tower is another story. I manage to climb up part of the bougainvillea – Ouch! – and then throw myself on to a small ledge.

When I've finally got my balance back I look up – I don't look down for dear life – and see the top of the flagpole. I toss my tie, lasso-style, towards it. I do this three times, and the third time I capture my target.

Mission accomplished, I climb down, leaving a good portion of my genetic material from my hands and knees on the gutters and drainpipes.

Sebastian and the gang are waiting for me at the bottom. They check out my hands and knees and the gashes on my arms from the bougainvillea thorns. 'Awesome!' they say. 'Who's next?'

Sebastian looks at me and I look at Sebastian and he knows he has to be the one, but he doesn't look so brave any more.

Sebastian follows in my footsteps – up the first drain-pipe and then up the second to Mrs Ho's classroom. He doesn't wave at Melly and Sam Ho either. It's touch and go as to whether he's going to duck inside her window and call it a day, but we jeer and cheer him on up the next drainpipe. He's halfway up when the drainpipe starts tearing away from the wall, but Sebastian's too quick to get caught out and makes it on to the ledge before he comes crashing down with the pipe. But it's then that he makes his first mistake: he looks down. Then he wobbles on the ledge and looks down again. I think I'm going to be sick. I think Sebastian is going to hurl too. 'Look up, Bas, look up,' I shout as loud as I can.

Sebastian needs to pull himself up from the ledge and on to the roof. But Sebastian looks down again and he falls.

He falls off the ledge and past the crooked drainpipe. His hands snatch at the air and I can hear the fabric of his trousers rip as he flails and bounces past Mrs Ho's window. Then his hands reach out and he's clinging to the ledge as his legs slam and splinter against the school wall. He's clinging on for dear life.

Before anyone can shout 'Don't break your neck!', the entire quad has joined me and my gang screaming up at the window. And Mrs Ho. She's standing at the edge of the crowd and her face is as white as any member of Vertigos Anonymous can be.

We stand and watch Sebastian clinging to the ledge. Then we watch Melly and Sam Ho peer out of Mrs Ho's classroom window to see what all the fun is about.

Sebastian doesn't have the strength to pull himself up on to the ledge. His feet can't find purchase against the bricks. I think if Sebastian's not very lucky he's going to be on crutches for the next ten years.

Then I see a crutch being lowered out of Mrs Ho's window and Sam Ho is holding Melly around the waist and she's leaning out of the window towards Sebastian. 'Grab on tight. Grab on, Bas,' I yell.

Sebastian grabs on to the crutch with one hand and then he lets go of the ledge to grab the crutch with two hands.

I see Melly straining forward until her little body is halfway out of the window. Her face is blue and she's gasping with the effort of trying to haul Sebastian on to the ledge.

It is in that moment that I see the last three weeks of Trinity College flash past my eyes: I see Melly panting as she introduces herself to me on the first day. I see her painting her nails with Tipp-Ex while Finger goes AWOL. I see her typing out my punishment essay and covering my books in brown paper and giving me *New Moon* to make me feel better when Mrs Ho beats up on me for bunking.

I see Melly letting me blow up balloons with her oxygen tank and frying in the sun on the lilo and buying me a school uniform – and the tie which is fluttering on top of the flagpole, signalling my expulsion from Trinity College.

I see Melly waiting to meet me every morning before school and I see myself walking past her towards Sebastian, shrugging her off.

'Hold on, Sam Ho. Hold Melly tight,' I scream.

Then Melly is three-quarters of the way out of the window and Sam Ho's face looks like Jacob the werewolf in *New Moon*, about to burst out of its skin with the effort of holding on to Melly.

I see Melly's face outside the boys' toilets as Sebastian gouges a hole in her bright pink hand, as she begs me to make him stop. I imagine the Tazz on the highway hitting the oil tanker going too fast. And I know there has to be a choice. Only one of them can fall.

I decide. 'Let go, Melly, let Sebastian go. You have to let him go,' I yell.

She looks at me, and I can see in her eyes that she can't believe me. She can't believe that it's her I want to save. Her bright pink hands still cling to the crutch.

Then I watch Sam Ho lose his grip on Melly and both Sebastian and Melly come tumbling down.

Cold Fact No. 14

In New York the penalty for jumping off a building is death. But in a pending bill, people who leap off structures of more than fifty feet without a permit would face up to a year in prison and a thousand-dollar fine.

Sixteen

I'm swinging as high as I can in the park. But as hard as I try, I just can't come short and hit the concrete below me.

It's the day after Sebastian and Melly fell two storeys down at the force of two students of average mass travelling at increasing velocity, accelerated by the gravitational pull of the cobbled quad below.

The tramp man is watching me from his spot by the trampoline. 'You're not looking so lekker today,' he says. 'Where are your gabbas?'

I tell him that Melly's in hospital with concussion and a sprained ankle. While she's there they're doing some tests on her to try and find out why she's a mouth-breather and suffers from sleep apnoea.

'And the crazy one? The boy with the orange hair?'

I tell him that Sebastian's also in hospital with a shattered thigh bone in one leg and a broken ankle in the other.

'So what are you doing here?' he asks me. 'Why aren't you at the hospital, visiting your chinas?' Then he looks at my school uniform and adds, 'And if you're not there, then why aren't you in school?'

I tell him that I treated the best friend a girl could ever have like rubbish and then, because I was acting like an idiot, she fell out of a window and hurt herself. I'm to blame. I feel so, so ashamed. My friend Melly must hate me as much as I hate myself.

I feel weird talking to the tramp man as he sucks away at his bottle of smelly grape juice. I'm not sure how much he understands, but somehow I end up telling him the whole story.

I tell him how I got off on the wrong foot with Mrs Ho on the first day at my new good school. And how I fell in with a bad influence and got dragged down. And how I've messed up my bursary and am probably going to get expelled for decorating the flagpole with my school tie.

I tell him how Fluffy lost his job at the newspaper last year and has a terrible, terrible life driving a tow truck (where he sees things that only God and his angels should ever see) and is in danger of losing his soul and getting fish eyes like Sharleen. And now he has a new best friend called Julia, and they're ten-to-one glad I have to go back to Pretoria to live with Mum and Sarel the Tick and go to a rubbish school.

I give him one of Fluffy's cards from Willie's Wreckers in case he ever gets lucky enough to own a car and unlucky enough to have a skid on the freeway.

The tramp man says that sometimes people make mistakes. Some of them make big mistakes. They DWD (Drive While Drunk) and kill their children and fall apart and come to live in a park and try and drink themselves to death. Then he says, 'Cheers!' and takes another swig from his bottle.

I offer him one of my polony sandwiches and he tells me that sometimes people just take a wrong turn and dent the front of their cars and get a traffic fine for not watching where they're going. 'Sometimes you just need to slow down and change direction,' he says.

I tell him that it's too late. I've lost my bursary and I've lost my best friend Melly.

He says it's never too late to choose the right road. 'Use your brains, girl,' he tells me. 'Put your seat belt on and hit the road.'

I get home and Mom and Sarel are there. I tell Mom I've come home to pack my bags. I've forfeited my bursary and my best friend Melly and I'm coming to live with her and Sarel in Pretoria.

'What the heck is going on, May?' Mom asks. She and Sarel have just popped over to leave me a present. She gives it to me. It's an iPod. Sarel says that this is the cheaper version, he has a more expensive one waiting for me in Pretoria for when I come to visit.

'In that case I'll leave the cheap one here,' I tell him, 'because I'm coming back with you now.'

'What the heck is going on, May?' Mom asks again.

I tell her the whole long story while Sarel washes his hands in the bathroom, leaving the door wide open for just in case.

Mom shakes her head and says that in her line of business she tells people lies all the time to make them feel better. And that there are a hundred different ways she could spin things to make me feel OK again. But the facts of the matter are that I've well and truly messed up. 'Stop acting dumb and perform to your potential, May,' she says.

I tell Mom that nothing's going to bring my bursary back. I don't need Alice the fortune-teller from *Twilight* or Jonathan Cainer to tell me that it's a done deal – it's over.

'Well, what's done is done,' Mom says. 'There's nothing you can do about your bursary, but you can make good with Melly. You can make your friendship better.'

'That's easier said than done,' I tell her. 'How the heck am I going to do that? Melly hates me.'

'You're smart,' Mom says. 'You'll think of something.'

Sarel and Mom leave me and I try to get my left and right brains working as a team for a change. I start by

154

writing a letter to Fluffy, saying sorry for messing up. Then I write one to Mrs Ho, telling her that I don't blame her for getting me skopped back to my rubbish school in Pretoria and that she must give my bursary to one of the other two hundred and fifty-nine kids who deserve it.

Finally I write a letter to Melly. I tell her why she's the best friend a girl could ever have. She's steadfast and loyal for not quitting on me when I got dragged down by Sebastian. She's brave and clever and generous and smart and I tell her that I even like the way she breathes on me and that I think her bright pink hands are original.

I put Melly's letter in an envelope and write *My Best Friend, Melly* on the front. Then I go and pack my bags and catch a taxi to Pretoria.

The next day Mom drags me back to Jozi. She tells me that I won't make things better by running away. 'And believe me, I know what I'm talking about,' she says.

The tow truck is parked outside the house next to the Toyota Corolla. Mom parks in the road and tells me to go on ahead, she needs to make a quick call. She sees my face and says, 'No, May, you need to do this on your own. I'll come now-now.'

Fluffy is sitting at the kitchen table. His hair is all mashed up and he's on his third cup of rooibos (though there are no Texan Plains in sight).

I sit down and Fluffy tells me that all is not lost. The School Board is meeting tomorrow about my bursary, but there are a couple of people who will speak up for me. Mrs Ho lifts her head from inside a dirty pot at the sink and says she's one of them. And there's Sam Ho and Fluffy and Melly. Things are not as dire as they appear.

Fluffy says that he's decided to do a three-point turn out of the cul-de-sac he's been trapped in these past three months. He got a call from someone he met on the job at Willie's Wreckers about a career as a stock-control manager in a travel agency. He's probably going to have to start at the bottom again, but at least he'll be going in the right direction.

'And at least you get to keep your soul,' I tell him.

He says the bonus is that he'll get to miss rush-hour traffic and work decent hours.

I ask him what the travel agency is called and Fluffy tells me it's called Swallows and Sons – which is as good a name for a funeral parlour as any.

Mom comes inside and overhears our exchange. 'Blinking grave digger,' she mutters under her breath.

Mom gives Mrs Ho a look from head to toe and then Fluffy introduces them. Mrs Ho gives Mom a look from toe to head and they sniff at each other. I say I need to head out into the garden for some fresh air.

Sam Ho and Melly are playing hopscotch in the yard.

Melly's a whizz on her crutches and she's giving Sam Ho a real run for his money. I watch them play for a while and then Melly sees me. She asks me if I want to play.

I ask her if it's dangerous. 'Will I bleed?'

Melly says she's afraid not, but it's fun.

I ask her if she's sure she wants me to play.

Melly says she's sure. Mrs Ho gave her a copy of the essay I wrote before I ran away to Pretoria: *My Best Friend, Melly*. Mrs Ho's going to enter it into the creative writing competition. 'Though one day I won't have bright pink hands any more,' she says. 'When they fix my lung I may not be so original.'

I tell her I'll take her oxygen tank as compensation.

Melly says I'm certain to win the competition and go to Forks, Washington and get to meet Stephenie Meyer and hang out with Edward the vampire.

I tell Melly that I don't care about winning any competition. I don't care about Stephenie Meyer and Bella or Edward the vampire or even Sebastian. She's the best friend a girl could ever want, pink hands or no pink hands.

Melly asks me if I'm sure.

'I'm sure,' I say.

Melly says let's play. And she gives me her crutches.

But I feel like I've won already.

In my experience, there are two kinds of families in this world.

There's the kind with a mother and father who love each other and their kids more than anything else in the whole wide world. They live together and get on each other's nerves. They fight sometimes and make up and get along as best they can. When one of them gets in trouble, the whole family pulls together and is there, one hundred per cent, to try and make things better. I've read about this sort of family. It's not mine.

The other kind is one where your parents get together and then take a wrong turn and end up splitting. And they split you in half too. You get to live with your father while your mother moves on and gets a life with Sarel in Pretoria. When you mess up, a whole bunch of people come together. They don't share your genes or your blood but they are one hundred per cent there for you. And they convince the School

Board as to why they should give you another chance to keep your bursary.

These people claimed me and became my kind of family. Different but mine.

It's Fluffy and Sam Ho. And Melly, Mrs Ho and me.

Acknowledgements

I would like to thank Hot Key for welcoming me so warmly to my new home and for doing what they do so brilliantly; Tina Betts, James Woodhouse and Reneé Naude for helping to make this book happen; Mike, Emily, Sophie and Jack for doing a lot of other things; and some teachers I have known, and others I don't, for doing their jobs and so much more.

If you ever met April-May in the flesh, you may not always understand what she's saying – even when she's speaking English. There are eleven official languages in South Africa and she likes to borrow words from all of them. And of course there's always South African slang. Here are some of the unfamiliar words you may have noticed in A MONTH WITH APRIL-MAY.

bakkie pick-up truck

bergie tramp, homeless person

biltong dried meat, similar to jerky

bladdie voetsak bloody go away

bliksemming cursing; literally, hitting

chinas friends

dof dumb, stupid

donder whack, as in whack on the back; also hit

gabbas friends

Gautrain high-speed railway service between Johannesburg and Pretoria

hamba-suka go away (from the Zulu words for 'go', *hamba*, and 'away', *suka*)

hold nickies/nickies my fingers cross fingers

Jozi Johannesburg

kombi camper van or minibus

Koo a South African producer of canned fruit, jam, beans and vegetables

lekker good, enjoyable, nice, sweet

polony spam-like sausage

puddysticks dead easy

Ricoffy a brand of coffee (chicory based, very cheap and popular in South Africa)

rooibos redbush tea (a herbal brew made from the South African *rooibos* shrub)

schloeps teacher's pets

skopped kicked out, sent packing

takkies trainers

Read on for an extract of the wonderful sequel to

A Month with April-May:

100 Days of April-May

The Eighth Story

There are only seven stories in the world, it is said.

You get the tragedy, where it all ends badly for the hero, the comedy, with a happy ending, and then there's the story where you take on a monster. You also have the tale about a voyage, where you leave as one person and return knowing a bit more about yourself, and the quest, where you find something or someone of great value. And then there's the rags-to-riches story, and, finally, the one about rebirth, where the central character finds a new reason for living.

But sometimes the story is a hodgepodge of all seven of these. It is the eighth story.

In my Grade Nine year at Trinity College I got caught up in a muddle of a tale. Tossed into this jumble were three people: a fat boy who ate himself silly because he felt worthless and angry, a kid who told lies because he was scared to face the truth and a useless shrink with a blind dog who couldn't help anyone because he didn't know how to help himself.

And then there was me – April-May February. Fourteen years old going on fifteen – the child of a divorced dad called Fluffy and a mom called Glorette. And my best friend, Melly, the girl who breathed through her mouth. And a golden boy with pale-green eyes called Sebastian, who made me stupid.

Our story could have ended any one of the seven ways that are set down for us. Or it could have had the other ending that goes with the eighth story.

In the beginning we didn't know how things would turn out. It all came down to the choices we made and the different roads we took towards our destiny.

In the end it all happened the way it did because of Melly, Fatty and me.

A boring or contemptible person or the foul emission of wind.

One

The Big Fart

It's all Melly's fault. She's one hundred per cent to blame for landing me with Fatty. If she'd been around it wouldn't have happened. None of it.

It's the first day of my Grade Nine year at Trinity College. I am seated at the back of the classroom with my head buried in a crossword puzzle. The clue for six letters across is: *Missing.* I scribble *ABSENT* on the page and look at the seat next to me. It's empty. *VACANT.*

My best friend Melly is away this term. She's having an operation on her lungs at Groote Schuur Hospital in Cape Town to make her breathe like a normal person. She left yesterday, panting all over me through her mouth. 'Please don't mess up while I'm away, April-May. Try to keep your head down and your mouth shut,' Melly said.

I told her that I always keep my mouth shut – she's the one who can't breathe though her nose.

Melly presented me with a bracelet made from a piece of leather and five ceramic beads which read: *WWMD?* (What Would Melly Do?) She says that if I'm ever in a tricky situation I must look at my wrist, pause, and consider my actions before leaping into boiling water. Melly's only been absent a day and I miss her badly. I feel *HOLLOW* (six letters).

Around me everyone's talking about their summer vacations. Plett and Umhlanga and Mauritius and Cape Town. And skiing in Austria. No one bothers to ask the bursary kid – that's me – what I did for the holidays, so I don't tell them that I was helping Fluffy with stock management at his travel agency.

Fluffy's my dad and he works at a funeral parlour called Swallows and Sons. He's in charge of the stock – what comes in, how long it stays and when it gets dispatched on its travels.

Controlling the stock takes a bit of juggling. Too much inventory creates space problems. Too little affects the end-of-the-month incentive bonus. And then there's the shelf life to consider. Fluffy says his clients are just like full-cream milk. If you don't keep a beady eye they'll go off and smell funny.

I toss the crossword puzzle aside and stand up as the

teacher arrives. He introduces himself as Dr Gainsborough and then shouts, 'Sit!'

The class sits and so does a dog. It's a golden retriever and it parks itself under the desk at Dr Gainsborough's feet. He says, 'Good girl!' and tells us that he is our homeroom teacher for the year. He also doubles as the Life Orientation teacher and the school psychologist. The Shrink. The person who deals with the crazy kids.

Dr Gainsborough then points to the dog at his feet. 'This is Emily,' he tells us.

Emily pricks up her ears and thumps her tail on the floor when she hears her name. Emily, it turns out, is blind. Dr Gainsborough hadn't known it when he picked her from a litter of seven SPCA puppies two years earlier. But when he discovered her visually challenged status it was too late to give her back – she was family. He pats Emily on the top of her head to reassure her of their kinship.

Dr Gainsborough takes out the register and calls our names. He soon gets to me, and I stand. 'So, this is you,' he says, as though recalling a fond memory. I tell him it is and he says, 'Fascinating. I've heard a lot about you.' He says this with a kindly glint in his eyes.

I've got a strange sort of celebrity status at Trinity College. I'm the girl who almost got expelled last year for attaching her tie to the school clock tower. And whose antics caused two pupils to nearly kill themselves by falling off the school roof, one of whom was my own dear Melly.

The other roof casualty was Sebastian, a boy with lime-green eyes who stole away from Trinity College soon after the incident, taking with him a slice of my cardiac muscle tissue.

I sit down and Dr Gainsborough comes to the end of the register. 'Ericca Ntona,' he says and looks up.

No one responds.

He tries again: 'Ericca Ntona.'

Dr Gainsborough is making an absent mark on the register when there's a knock at the door and the school secretary pokes her head into the classroom. 'So sorry to disturb,' she says. She's got a new kid with her. He arrived late and got a bit lost. She stands back from the doorway and the new kid walks into the room.

Walks is an understatement. He lumbers in, pulling his large body behind him. He is the biggest kid I have ever seen. He is about ten feet tall and ten feet wide with a face as dark and heavy as one of our famous Jozi summer thunderclouds. I can't take my eyes off this supersized kid.

There's a rude whistle from the middle of the room and Emily gives a little yelp. Whispers shoot across the room like sniper fire: 'lardass', 'jelly-belly', 'Buddha-butt', 'gross'. The mean kids toss words around the room like a bunch of delegates at a Crossword Puzzle Convention trying to determine the solution for *Obese insult*. They settle on a name: *FATTY* (five across). That's what he'll be called from now on. It is decided.

'This is Ericca Ntona,' the secretary says to Dr Gainsborough. 'The new bursary kid.'

Dr Gainsborough frowns at the secretary, looks down at his register and then up at Fatty. 'Ericca?' he says. 'It's Eric, surely?' He strokes the tips of his white goatee and peers uncertainly at Fatty through his pebble spectacles.

Fatty glowers and Dr Gainsborough swallows hard. 'Of course it's Ericca. And why not,' he says.

There are more sniggers from my classmates. 'Fatty, Fatty, Fatty,' they whisper.

I put my head down as the heat creeps up my neck. I know about dumb names. I'm April-May February. The calendar girl. But compared to Ericca Ntona, I got off lightly.

Dr Gainsborough looks around the classroom for a spare desk. I squeeze my thumbs in my fists until I hear the knuckles crack. *Not me, not me*, I beg the gods. *Please, not me*.

Dr Gainsborough points to the back of the classroom. At me. Fatty is going to be my new desk-mate for the term.

Come back, Melly, I yell inside my head. I'm getting landed with the fat boy with a mad-bad face and a girl's name.

173

Fatty barrels his way past the desks and throws his satchel down on the floor. Then he dumps himself into the chair next to me. As he settles, he lifts the desk two feet off the ground with his knees. I make myself as small as possible as he spreads his meaty arms across the desk.

Dr Gainsborough says that our lesson today will take the form of a short essay: 'My Family and Me'. He wants to know who we are. Get to know us, as it were. As he says this he reaches down under his desk and scratches Emily's ear.

I remember how weird I felt at the beginning of last year, coming to Trinity College on a bursary and not having any friends. I recall how Melly wheezed all over me within the first five minutes as she claimed me as her soul mate.

I take a deep breath in (not out), get out my exam pad and offer Fatty a sheet of paper. He reaches out. His hands are small; his fingers slender with nails as white as toothpaste. 'My name is April-May February,' I whisper.

Fatty looks at me and glares. He thinks I'm mocking him by making a stupid name joke. He drops his hand and turns away. I try and explain, but it comes out all wrong. It's hard to make clear to someone you've just met that your parents were at odds from the day you were born. That they liked different seasons and couldn't agree on which month to call me. I give up trying to set things straight and get on with my essay.

174

Fatty gets an asthma pump out of his blazer pocket and sucks on it hard. Then he gets an exam pad from his satchel. And a lunch box. While he writes he guzzles away at its contents: sandwiches like bricks filled with last night's stew.

I write my essay, ignoring the deep breathing and chomping going on next to me. I tell Dr Gainsborough all about my family. There's Fluffy, who is a stock control executive at a travel agency, and his best friend and intimate other, Julia Ho, who is the deputy principal at Trinity College. Then there is Just Sam Ho, Julia's eight-year-old son who drives me mental most days but is also sort of okay. And last and best there's Melly, my special friend, who is more of a sister to me and who has problems in the respiratory department. That's my family. I stop there.

I doodle a bit on my desk and then I write my last sentences: *I have a birth mother called Glorette. She tells a lot of lies and is having a baby with her new husband, Sarel the Bloodsucker, in six months' time.* Enough said.

Fatty has finished the contents of his lunch box and makes a loud burp. The smell wafts over me. Lamb stew and onions. Then he shuffles about and lifts a large buttock off the seat.

I know that move. A burp's one thing but there's no ways I'm standing for an almighty blast from the dark recesses of Fatty's large intestine.

I stand up. 'Don't you dare try and rip one near me, you fat pig,' I scream with the kind of lung capacity that Melly can only dream of. But as soon as the words are out of my mouth I want to shred my tongue and pickle it in shame.

Dr Gainsborough looks up and Emily starts howling. 'That is enough. Sit down!' His voice trembles with outrage.

I sit down, trying to keep my distance from Fatty, who has bowed his head and wrapped his arms around his chest. He is sucking on his asthma pump like he's never going to see another birthday.

The class hoots with laughter and peers around at Fatty and me as Dr Gainsborough gets up from his desk. 'Stay!' he commands Emily as he strides to the back of the classroom.

'I will not tolerate the shouting of insults in my personal space,' Dr Gainsborough barks, arriving in front of my desk and looking down at me with eyes that are no longer kindly. 'I will not have one student destabilising the emotional autonomy of another. Do you understand?'

I nod. Three nods. Which means I understand. And I feel really bad. About what I said.

Then Dr Gainsborough lifts the lunch box off my desk and frowns at me with eyes that tell me he thinks I'm some trouble-causing guzzler. 'Eating in class is against the rules.'

I swallow my tongue and wait for Fatty to own up. But he rasps in staccato time with my beating heart and says nothing. And lets me take the rap.

'Eating in class gets you an afternoon's detention. This afternoon. In my classroom. Straight after school. Do you understand?'

I nod. Four nods. Which means that I understand that Fatty has got me detention. On my first day. And I feel really mad. About what Fatty failed to fess up to.

'Finished your essay?' Dr Gainsborough asks me.

I give him my essay.

'Finished your essay?' he asks Fatty.

As Fatty tears the page out of his exam pad and hands it to Dr Gainsborough I catch a glimpse of a part of the line at the top of the page. It says: *I have no mother* . . .

Dr Gainsborough marches back to his desk and I look at my Melly bracelet. What Would Melly Do? My Melly would write the detention off as a little misunderstanding. She would become best friends (second best after me) with this sad, fat, hungry, silent, motherless orphan. She would breathe all over him and say, 'I can see that we are going to be the best of friends despite your antisocial habits.' That's what Melly would do.

I know Melly's way is the right way. The only way.

But I close my eyes to Melly's bracelet and lean over towards Fatty and say, 'You got me in trouble, you weasel.

I've got detention because of you. So from now on, dude, you just stay out of my way.'

Fatty says nothing, but I can see from the daggers drawn in the black holes of his eyes that he's got the message.

Two

Shacking Up

My father, Fluffy, and his intimate other, Julia Ho, are hunched over the kitchen table when I arrive at Chez Matchbox, the place I also call Home.

Fluffy is in a state of huge excitement. He is jabbing away at a piece of paper, scribbling and crossing out and adding up sums like a psychotic accountant on a double-espresso binge. 'I think I can just afford it,' he says as I walk in, mashing his huge tangle of hair into a billion knots.

'What can we just afford?' I ask him. Meat three times

a week would be a nice start. Or the Interweb. And a computer to go with it.

He tells me that we're going to be doing some building. We are going to convert the garage into a bedroom and en-suite bathroom.

I throw my arms around Fluffy's neck. How did he know? Number One on my wish list is to have my own private bathroom and not have to share bath scum with Fluffy. It's a dead tie with a computer. And the Interweb.

Fluffy says that he's also excited. In five months' time thousands of footie fans are going to descend on the country, looking for a place to call home for the duration of the Soccer World Cup. And Chez Matchbox, with its new en-suite, will become this place for some homeless member of the European Community.

'Everyone's doing it,' Fluffy explains. South Africans everywhere are preparing to fleece the foreigners and make a killing on the back of the soccer madness. So why not him? If the euro holds up, the rent from the room will more than pay off the building costs and fund a holiday in Margate.

Mrs Ho is studying Fluffy's figures. 'This will mean a second bond. Is that wise, July? In this economic climate?'

What Mrs Ho means is Fluffy's economic climate. The one that he has been stuck in since he got retrenched from his newspaper job more than a year ago and began working in the dead people industry – first driving a tow truck for Willie's Wreckers and now working in a funeral parlour.

I hear the words *second bond* and I see *LOAN. ALBATROSS. DEBT.* Something Fluffy excels at getting himself into. Already his pay cheque barely touches sides. We can hardly meet the monthly payments on the one bond. A second bond is Bad News, and I tell Fluffy precisely this using these two words.

Fluffy says that I must think positive. People should have the confidence to make their own luck. In return I tell Fluffy that I think affirming thoughts about our bond and my destiny all the time. Every month I send karmic blessings to the Governor of the Reserve Bank, trying to make her drop the interest rate. A percentage point drop means a tiny stash of cash for the Rainy-Day Tin. A rise means two-minute noodles for the month.

Mrs Ho places a cautious hand on Fluffy's arm. 'July, can we talk about this? I have a few thoughts.'

Fluffy glances up and catches the look on Mrs Ho's face. It's an expression that he has learned to read during the past year that they have been steady intimates. It means that she wants to talk to him in private.

Fluffy tells me to go and do my homework. I reply that I finished it all during my afternoon's detention and that he's not to worry, I'm happy to hang out with him and Mrs Ho and chat.

Mrs Ho's eyebrows leap into her hairline like angry question marks. 'Detention?' she queries. Fluffy punishes his hair. 'Detention!' he exclaims.

I bite my tongue in two and say that I think I should go and clean the bathroom. And tidy my room. And tidy Fluffy's bedroom too.

Fluffy says, 'Oh no you don't, young lady, sit down.' And they subject me to verbal waterboarding until I explain how Fatty's (I call him Ericca Ntona) antisocial habits caused me to express myself in a loud and emotionally incontinent manner. Yes, I called the new bursary kid a fat pig.

Fluffy and Mrs Ho give me looks full of reproach. Looks I can read because I have known Fluffy for nearly fifteen years, and Mrs Ho for more than one year, which is long enough for me to know her 'I'm so, so disappointed in you, April-May' look.

I tell them that they've got me wrong. I'm a chubby chum. I love fleshy people. There's Ishmael – Fluffy's best friend next to Mrs Ho – who drives a tow truck for Willie's Wreckers. He's got more shares in the blubber department than an obese whale, and I like him just as well as thin people. And I am also inordinately fond of pigs, who are the cleanest animals on Planet Earth, even though they will eat just about anything and make bad smells. Like Ericca Ntona (Fatty).

I start backing out of the kitchen before I stuff both feet into my mouth, leaving the two of them shaking their heads.

In my bedroom I find Sam Ho lolling on my bed. He's fiddling with my cellphone and listening to my music on my iPod. An open bottle of nail varnish on my bedside table next to a half-painted wooden toy is proof that he's been in my cupboards. Again.

He doesn't see me enter the bedroom. Nor does he see me pull the duvet from under him, an action which dumps him on the floor. I grab my stuff and drag him by one ankle towards the door and chuck him out.

There are two things worth mentioning about Sam Ho. The first is that he belongs to Mrs Ho. The second thing is that while I think he's okay for an eight-year-old troll, mostly he's an annoying brat who should stay out my room.

Sam Ho hobbles down the passage towards the kitchen, squealing like a stuck pig – a stuck goat. I make a mental memo to ban the pig word from my daily discourse. It's a three-lettered stink bomb.

Sam Ho is hobbling because he hurt his back in a car accident some time ago. It caused the loss of a family member – his father – and damaged his spine. He was on crutches for most of last year and is still learning to adjust to putting one foot in front of the other instead of swinging and swaying on crutches.

He is also hobbling because it is guaranteed to score sympathy points with Fluffy and get me in trouble for beating up on him.

I follow Sam Ho towards the kitchen – intent on damage limitation – and catch the tail-end of the conversation. 'Moving in with April and me would make us a real family.' Then there's a pause and I conclude from the slobbery silence that Fluffy and Mrs Ho are having a romantic moment across the tomato sauce.

Which Sam Ho and I put a very sharp stop to with our appearance.

Mrs Ho tells Sam Ho to hush, please, love, stop squealing because we are having an adult confab about some life-changing issues.

'If Julia moves in with us,' Fluffy explains, 'then she could rent out her house.'

The cash would help Fluffy pay off the building loan, and the two of them would recoup the damage and split the huge profits on his rent-the-en-suite-to-affluent-soccer-tourist scheme.

Fluffy is flushed. He looks like he's won the Lotto.

'But where would she sleep?' I make squiggly eyebrows in Mrs Ho's direction. Somebody's got to ask the question. And I'm still smarting over them chewing my ear off about Fatty. I'm not going to make things too easy for them.

Chez Matchbox boasts two bedrooms. One is Fluffy's and

the other is mine. Fluffy flushes some more. Then he blushes over his flushes while Mrs Ho starts shredding her cuticles.

'Of course Julia will share my bedroom with me,' Fluffy finally says.

I'm a grown-up sort of a girl with a mind as broad as Fatty's butt. I know all about the facts of life and the physical goings on between two people who have declared themselves in love and are committed to an intimate partnership. 'Of course she will,' I say to Fluffy. 'But where will Sam Ho stay if you rent out his house?'

Twenty minutes later I am storming down the road in the direction of Melly's house with a satchel containing most of my worldly possessions. Sam Ho to share a bedroom with me? Is that where the thinking is going? Is that what Fluffy means by of course Sam Ho will live with us? I'd prefer to share a bedroom with a pig. Or Fatty.

I'm halfway to Melly's house when I remember that she's not there. She's in Cape Town, having her lung butchered to help her breathe like a normal person. I backtrack to the park across the road from my school. It's a favourite hang-out of mine.

A couple of kids are on the see-saw, so I head for the trampoline. I jump high. So high that I can see over the palisade fence, across the road and into the school soccer field.

Some kids are kicking a couple of soccer balls around. The goalie is totally rubbish. He's sitting on the grass in front of the goalposts with his head in his hands. And as the balls hit him, he hunches over as if he is trying to protect himself rather than save the ball. Lazy old thing.

Then I see that the kids are using the lazy goalie as a target. And the harder the balls hit the bowed figure, the louder they laugh.

Call me a nosy parker, or meddlesome or even a snoop, but there is one thing I can't abide, and that's bullies.

'Hey! Stop that!' I shout, and then I quit jumping and get my satchel. My cellphone has thirty text messages but I don't bother to read them because I know it's just Fluffy saying *Please, come home, April. Please, come home so we can talk.*

I run out of the park and head towards the school sports fields. I peer through the fence and watch as the mean kids continue slamming those balls at the crouching figure on the grass.

Then, before I can shout stop right away else I'll come over and kick those soccer balls into the backs of your throats, the stooped figure gets up. The kids jeer and whistle and a couple of the scaredy-cats start running away. This makes me smile wide. Run, you cowardly custards. Run, you yellow-bellied bullies, run. I laugh as they run.

Then I recognise the goalie. It's Fatty. He lumbers towards the side of the field, his head down, wheezing. And then he looks up and sees me. Standing there laughing. And I can see from the dark expression that crosses his face that he thinks I'm part of this mean game. And that I've been watching and laughing all this time while the other kids jeered and beat up on him.

Q & A with Edyth Bulbring

What inspires your writing?

The people who inspire me to write are the people I meet every day, like Trevor and Phineus, my builders. I am inspired by an elderly Portuguese dressmaker called Louisa who made my daughter's matric dance dress. And then, apart from people like Louisa, I am constantly moved to write by the people I love most in the world – my family. My two teenage daughters and son drive me mental most of the time but when they aren't doing that I am constantly in awe as to how funny and clever and nice they are. And then the children's father says many things that inspire me to write, things like: 'Why don't you write a book that earns some decent cash?' and 'If you can't write a book that sells do you think you could learn how to cook?' Stuff like that – really inspirational.

What has been the most exciting moment of your career so far?

When I heard that someone wanted to publish my book, *The Summer of Toffie and Grummer* (published by OUP in South Africa), which was the second book I wrote, I didn't celebrate. I cried. By then I had written four books no one wanted to publish and I was feeling like a real loser. So I was very relieved. Then all the others got published so I was even more relieved and did some more crying.

How did you first become an author?

I went to university and studied history and politics and got a part-time job as a switchboard operator at a newspaper. But I was useless at it so they let me write a few stories. I ended up being the political correspondent for the *Sunday Times*, a newspaper in South Africa. But along the way while I was being a journalist I had three children and one day I decided to stay at home and look after them. I didn't know what else to do when they were at school so I decided to write a book for them. And when no one wanted to publish it, I wrote a few more books. And then they got published. I never really wanted to be a writer, I just wanted to tell stories to my children to make them laugh. It was my way of connecting with them. This is the reason why I write books. To shore up my memories. To tell the stories about the people I love. My books are for my children. They are my love letters that I hope will bind us together.

What was your earliest career aspiration?

I wanted to be an air hostess and travel the world. But in the days when I was young you had to be very tall and very pretty to be an air hostess. I was neither.

What advice would you give to budding writers?

I have a few rules. I love rules. It makes me feel that my life has some order. The first rule is: read, read, read and read some more. You can't write if you don't read. The second rule is: keep a diary. It should be about things that make you laugh or cry; people you meet, the things they say, things that interest you what you experience every day. It will give you material for your books. I kept a diary for many years when I was young and when I was pregnant with my first child I trashed them all because I thought I was going to die in childbirth and I didn't want anyone to read them. I regret trashing my diaries a lot. The third rule is: write every day – in your diary, on Facebook or on a blog. It will help you develop your voice. The fourth rule is: don't listen to what people say you should be writing. Write what you want to write about. They are your stories and you shouldn't try and write someone else's story. The last rule is: respect your readers. Don't try and lie to them or cheat them or give them rubbish.

What was your favourite childhood book?

I read everything I could lay my hands on and never really took note of who was writing them. I read all my mother's and sisters' library books. I read lots of trashy books and some good books too. I was a bit of a glutton. But my love of reading was not sparked by one particular book; it was newspapers that did it. Every morning I used to lie in bed between my mother and father while they read the newspapers. And I would point to some photo and ask my father what the story was. And he would tell me all about it. It was really special. Actually I lie – he used to say: 'For crying in a bucket, I'm trying to read my newspaper; give me some peace.' I couldn't wait to be able to read the stories behind the pictures for myself. That's what sparked my love for reading.

The children's books I really liked were written by Enid Blyton and Roald Dahl and Willard Price. But the one author I really like who writes for both adults and teens is Philip Pullman. I loved the *His Dark Materials* trilogy and I read these when I was an adult. They are cross-over books which I think are the best sort of novels. I loved *Anne of Green Gables* by Lucy Montgomery and I have tried to get my daughters to read it and they have refused. It breaks my heart. I suppose if I read it now I wouldn't like it much but I liked it then. The book gave me a real soft spot for girls with red hair.

Where is your favourite place to write?

I write in two places. The first place is at home in Johannesburg at my desk in my sort of study which leads on to my stoep. I find it easier to write when there is a lot of activity going on. So when I sit down to write a new book I usually also embark on a new building project on my house. Or I start a new garden project – ripping out old beds and planting new ones. So when I write I have lots of people coming and going and hammering and asking me to order sand and bricks which gets me very excited and energised. I also get to make the builders (Trevor and Phineus) tea and to chat about life and things.

The second place I write is at my cottage in Stanford, which is a village two hours from Cape Town. I take a week off from my family and sit and write on the stoep. I like this time away a lot as I don't have to cook or bath or get out of my pyjamas. I eat old Christmas cake and peanut butter and fish sandwiches. When I want to see people I go and buy Ghost Pops (crisps) and Coke at the cafe and talk to the people walking their dogs.

How do you read – print, digitally or both?

I read print books. I was given a Kindle for my birthday three months ago but I haven't used it yet. I buy most of my books from the Hospice bookshop down the road from me.

Who do you most admire?

I admire people who tell great stories. I go through stages of having huge crushes on authors and I devour them until someone else catches my eye, but I always go back to Jane Austen and she never disappoints. I love her irony and her sense of empathy. And her long sentences. I wish I could write long, complicated, grammatically perfect sentences. In terms of living people, I admire my two teenage daughters and my son. They have grown into wonderful people, despite me.

Are there any books you wish you had written?

There is one author who I esteem above all others for writing the best book ever written: Harper Lee (who only ever published one book and got it right the first time). Whenever I see *To Kill a Mockingbird* in charity shops, I buy it. I have about thirty copies and I'm going to keep on buying it. She inspires me to keep on writing until I get it right.

Edyth Bulbring

Edyth Bulbring was born in Boksburg, South Africa and grew up in Port Elizabeth. She attended the University of Cape Town where she completed a BA whilst editing the university newspaper *Varsity*. Having worked as a journalist for fifteen years, including time spent as the political correspondent at the *Sunday Times* of South Africa covering the first ever democratic elections, Edyth moved into writing full time. Edyth has published six books in South Africa and *A Month with April-May* is the first of her books to be published in the UK.